"A CODE OR DIE BY"

GEORGE WHATLEY

Copyright © 2020 by George Whatley

All right reserved. No part of this book may be used or reproduced by any means, graphic, electronic, or mechanical, including photocopying, recording, taping or by any information storage retrieval system without the written permission of the author except in the case of brief quotations embodies in critical article and reviews.

Because of the dynamic nature of the Internet, any web addresses or links contained in this book may have changed since publication and may no longer be valid. The reviews expressed in this work are solely those of the author and do not necessarily reflect the views of the publisher, and the publisher hereby disclaims any responsibility for them.

*With love to my wife Shirley
to celebrate just over 40 years together.*

Jeff has recently retired, after working in all the different aspects of banking security most of his life. He retired as head of security of an Iranian Bank in London, in contrast to this, in his spare time he was also a successful local fighting environmentalist. He lived with his wife Karen in a nice little bungalow in the Estuary.

Jeff and Karen had not long finished dinner together when the phone rang. Jeff answered it and spoke for a while. He put the telephone down, said to his wife Karen, "that was Bob, he's now changing the venue of the meeting for tomorrow, he can't make the meeting at the Estuary Community Centre.

We will have to meet at the Center on the Mainland, he said something about a major breakthrough and meeting someone important after our meeting".

Jeff then looked puzzled at Karen and said, "he asked me to bring that list of names that we have been working on, as he thinks it might be important, he was quite mysterious about it, he also said something very strange", he added, "he could not tell me over the phone as it wasn't a secure line, I've never heard him talk that way before it is quite mysterious".

Karen said, "perhaps it might be a breakthrough on the investigation of that major spill the Gas Terminal had at the now L.N.G. Terminal, the one they had a few years ago?".

"I still believe that was a big cover-up", Jeff replied, "I also believe Councillor Randle was up to his neck in it, for those findings to have come out, someone very powerful must have sat on the results of that investigation". Councillor Randle was opposed to Jeff leading and winning the Oil Refinery Fight a few years before. Councillor Randle was still an arch-enemy of Jeff's, they had clashed many times in public.

Karen was now referring to a major spill of Liquid Petroleum Gas at the Gas Terminal a few years ago in the Estuary. Jeff believed the company tried to cover up the major spill by not reporting it to the authorities so the history of their safety record was not compromised. He had a reliable source that told him about the ship to shore transfer that went wrong, causing the massive spill of 160 liquid metric tons of L.P.G. Jeff had reported it to the local council environmental department who were also the Hazardous Substance Authority, (H.S.A.) which was headed by Councillor Randle. Jeff believed Councillor Randle who was still an arch-enemy of Jeff's, headed that committee. Jeff still reported the incident, the department did not believe him, as the terminal had not reported to them any spill of any kind, and certainly not one as large as that, which could cause a major incident, plus the council would have to invoke it's emergency powers to safeguard the surrounding population and no one on the council's emergency team headed by Councillor Randle would make that decision in case it was a false alarm, so they did nothing preferring to believe the terminal management that there was not an incident, therefore, in turn, treating Jeff's report as hostile information.

When Jeff was told by the Council's Hazard Substance Authority they were doing nothing about his reported major spill, as they believed it to be a false statement by Jeff, he went above their heads and reported the incident to his contacts in the Health and Safety Executive, who did believe him.

The H.S.E. went to the terminal and did an instant site visit and inspection. The Health & Safety Inspectors found the information Jeff had provided was true.

Jeff had opened a can of worms that the Authorities did not want to be opened.

The investigation found a Bursting Disc which had failed during the ship to shore operation causing the spill of 163 liquid metric tons of L.P.G. which in turn formed an Unconfined Vapour Cloud of very volatile gas. This drifted over the site, then over the sea wall, and luckily dissipated over the sea of the Estuary.

The Bursting Disc which failed is a safety device designed to blow just before, or instead of, the major storage tank failing. This storage tank is as big as the Albert Hall. This is deemed to be the worst-case scenario that could happen at this type of terminal. An emergency plan has to be planned for and implemented if this type of incident happened.

In a part of the investigation by the H.S.E., it was found this Bursting Disc should be changed annually. The Bursting Disc that failed in that incident was 11 years old. The question arose about the lack of maintenance by the terminal management causing the failure of this Bursting Disc.

The failure of this Bursting Disc caused the massive spill of 163 liquid metric tons of Liquid Petroleum Gas (L, P, G,) which once open to the atmosphere gassed off into an expanding gas cloud of Petroleum gas it became an Unconfined Vapour Cloud of gas, luckily the Unconfined Gas Cloud drifted over the sea wall and out to sea with the wind. If the wind had been blowing in any other direction, the Unconfined Vapour Cloud would have found an ignition source on land. That scenario was unthinkable from the devastation that would have caused.

The investigation by the H.S.E. investigation found there was a number of failures to report, the failure to report the incident to the Emergency Services which was headed by Councillor Randle's department, the failure of the perimeter gas alarms that were not working, also the portable gas alarms were not working, apparently, the first the terminal control room knew about the major spill was when a member of staff coming on duty spotted the very large Unconfined Vapour Cloud (U.V.C.) drifting over the site of the terminal towards the sea wall and reported it to management, who then, in turn, tried to cover up the major incident up to save their safety record from being compromised.

The failure to report the incident to the local Hazardous Substance Authority which was Headed by Councillor Randle, who should have called the Emergency Services and evacuated the residence in the area, the council were reprimanded for ignoring the report from Jeff, because someone either, tried to cover it up, or there was a failure to grasp the magnitude of the danger of putting so many lives at risk. The incident highlighted the failure with the present system and its failure to respond in case of an alarm whether it was false or not.

Jeff had said to the Press at the time of the spill that if the gas cloud had drifted out over the Estuary and not out to sea and but over land which was the way the prevailing wind normally blew, plus had there been an ignition source present when that cloud of gas escaped, it would have been the biggest peacetime disaster ever known.

Jeff had made a lot of enemies that day. He just added them to the list he already had, from Councillor Randle, members of the Council who had tried to cover up the incident and the Terminal Management who tried to save their safety record by covering up the incident. Jeff had been ridiculed by the company, he had been called a sensationalistic scaremonger, an activist that was only trying to frighten people, everything was under control and the fact there had been no explosion proved that the terminal was safe, in turn, Jeff challenged the competence of the Management of the terminal.

Jeff argued back that the population relied on the Terminal Management being honest and reporting to the Emergency Authorities any major incidents that could affect the safety of any members of the outlying community. He said they had tried to cover up the major spill at the terminal to protect their safety record.

Jeff had come to the realization that the established Methane Gas Terminal posed the greatest threat to the community because of the substances being processed and the dangers that came with the process of storing and processing Liquid Natural Gas (L.N.G.)

Whilst Jeff knew, L.N.G. (Liquid Natural Gas) which was Methane Gas, was the type of gas used in everyone's household cookers, the danger to the community arises from the bad management of these terminals and of the processing and storage of this substance, this is because, L.N.G. is stored in liquid form by concentrating it down 620 times by refrigeration from gas to liquid. It is stored at temperatures of below Minus 160C or below Minus 270 F. The stored gas is so cryogenically cold in liquid form it would freeze-dry everything in its path.

Whilst there is a lot of technical detail, to the lay-man when the gas is required the L.N.G. liquid is warmed up, therefore expanding the liquid to a gas 620 times its volume, when the neat gas is mixed with air and is between 80% to 95% air to methane then pumped to the consumer.

The gas is transported and stored in its liquid form in giant double skin tanks, to the layman, they look like giant Thermos bottle-shaped tanks.

Originally the Estuary gas terminal was the first experimental storage facility of L.N.G. of its kind in the UK.

At the site of this first L.N.G. Terminal, they had in-ground tanks built that comprised of 4 large round pits dug into the clay type soil where they sealed a lid on the 4 round pits, then they would freeze the 4 round in-ground pits with cryogenically frozen liquid, therefore forming giant in-ground storage tanks.

In the new experimental in-ground storage tanks the terminal operators put the cryogenically cold L.N.G.

Over a number of years, because of having to keep the L.N.G. at cryogenically so low temperatures in clay soil, a major problem arose.

The clay soil that formed the in-ground tanks now storing the cryogenically cold Liquid Natural Gas started to crack and formed spreading fissures deep within the ground.

Over years the cracks increased the L.N.G. flowed into these deep spreading fissures, eventually, all the 4 tanks were interconnected via these fissures, therefore forming an ever-expanding permafrost, which in turn caused a 3-foot ground heave and further destabilized the area, in turn, threatened to destabilize the rest of the gas terminal.

This eventually affected the foundations of the above-ground tanks and processing plant. In the end, the in-ground storage tanks were dismantled at great cost and the site was cleaned up.

The Terminal changed hands to a company storing and processing a different type of gas, Liquid Petroleum Gas (L.P.G.) for a number of years they processed and stored L.P.G. and sold it in bottled form.

Karen interjected and said, "I, like you, don't trust them as terminals of this nature are only as safe as long as the management manages well. When you get bad or poor management, the site becomes a very dangerous site to the community, not only because of the nature of the substances being processed, but corners being cut to save costs and increase profit".

Jeff added to the conversation and said, "When that incident happened, I was surprised the management eventually admitted they were seeking Guidance from the H.S.E. as to what the management was to do next, as you know my retort was if they did not know then they should not be running this type of plant, my enemies were stacking up and being added too".

Karen said, "in the end, the H.S.E. took the Gas Company to court and they were fined for breaching H.S.E. regulations, mind you it will stay on their record the breach of regulations".

When Jeff found out this same company decided to revamp their plant and wanted to be processing and marketing L.N.G., Jeff led a successful fight to stop them.

This fight involved taking on the big boys again, in doing so, making more enemies.

The gas terminal proposal was, they would do the processing, a Japanese Company would be the bankers and the same Japanese company would supply the special gas ships to transport the L.N.G. to the U.K. terminal, and it would be distributed via a major player for the Nation Grid.

This was getting support from certain councillors with Councillor Randle leading the charge, but Jeff galvanized the people together once again and started the fight against the siting of L.N.G. close to a residential area.

Like during the Oil Refinery fight, Jeff also decided to hold a referendum, this had great support from the families in the Estuary, once again he used old sweet jars sealed with a slot cut in the lid, voting slips were given out and people could vote as to whether they wanted the threat of L.N.G. back in their lives. During this time in the campaign, Jeff heard the representatives from the two Japanese Companies were visiting the Gas terminal for a big important meeting.

Knowing the Japanese culture of they must never lose face, plus knowing the easiest way to access any building is to tailgate behind someone as they enter a premise, Jeff made sure he was at the terminal entrance when the delegation arrived.

As the stretch limousine with the Japanese delegation arrived at the terminal, security opened the electronic outer gates, Jeff tailgated the stretch limousine with the delegation on board, on the blind side of security.

The car stopped for security check, and the delegation got out of the limousine. Jeff approached the Japanese delegation bowed to them, handed them a jar plus a few voting slips, bowed and exited the terminal before the electronic gates closed, security was not aware he had entered the premises. The delegation carried the jar and voting slips into the very important meeting.

When the Japanese delegation was introduced and met the terminal management, the Japanese delegation wanted to know what to do with the jar and the voting slips. The Japanese delegation was embarrassed and lost face, also the embarrassed management was upset at their breach of security, plus they had to tell them about the opposition to the plans of siting L.N.G. on the site. Jeff had even more enemies stacking up.

A few days later the jar and voting slips were posted back to Jeff with a note saying the staff at the terminal could vote from their own houses, but Jeff heard from his contacts the management were furious over the incident.

"A Code to Live or Die by"

Jeff's mind was now preoccupied with the paperwork he had to get together and get sorted into the right order it was going to be a late night, plus he also needed to prepare the list on names for Bob he had been working on for quite some time.

The phone rang again this time Karen answered it. Jeff was so engrossed in getting the files together he only distantly heard her say it was one of her daughters. Jeff only half heard his wife speak to him. He was so engrossed in the paperwork he was preparing when she went to bed. When he followed later, she was fast asleep.

Jeff had a restless night, his mind kept running over that major spill at the terminal. He was still angry that the cover-up of the major spill had worked, and the company got away with a small fine. He also felt that the Whitehall mandarins had struck again by pulling the power strings they had, which in turn seemed to safeguard the power of the energy companies, and the local authority.

Jeff knew, as much as he tried to expose the situation, he was being buried by powerful people. These faceless people were not going to take the responsibility of protecting communities where the massive profits of the energy companies are concerned.

He knew how powerful these International companies were globally. They were so powerful they controlled countries economies.

He also knew this was the injustice that he fought against, but his local and national dignitaries were not listening. He felt they were too busy getting on the gravy train of power and profit.

Jeff felt it would take a disaster of biblical proportions for them to sit up and take notice of what was really going on. By then there would be the wringing of hands and platitudes, the people who would suffer would be the people that have to live and work within the shadow of these sites, these would be the victims.

Doug, a good friend to Jeff and one of his fellow campaigners, once said, "if you carry on the way you do, in trying to find and expose the corruption, you could find yourself in a concrete slab propping up a motorway".

Unfortunately, Doug had died in a police cell, the verdict was accidental death. Jeff tried to get to the bottom of it but came up against a solid brick wall of silence.

Little did Jeff know how close to the truth he was going to be, and that those principles that he had earned on the Bombsites of South London where he was born, that he held so dear during the Oil Refinery War, were going to be stretched to breaking point over the next few days.

The meeting with Bob was about the forthcoming public inquiry, they had been trying to look into the conflagration of high fire risk industries being planned all along the Estuary.

Jeff was representing the local residents as chairman of a group called "People Must Come First". The group was a non-political and non-violent group that was concerned about the dangers of the conflagration of the energy industry being sited close to residential areas.

Plus Jeff wanted to know how the latest planning application to expand the Gas Terminal had been so successful. Jeff felt there was a lot of underhandedness being carried out as the applications had been steam-rolled through at great speed and the public were not allowed to be represented or their argument heard because it was deemed to be in the "National Economic Interest" and the public concerns were over-ruled. Now Jeff was fighting to get another Inquiry so the people's concerns could be heard.

Jeff's friend Bob was short and stocky. He was the Chairman of another group of legal brains called "Legal Help for People" that assisted environmental groups put forward their case at public inquiries. At these sort of planning inquiries, the general public do not know what they can and can't say. All they know is they do not want it, but to be heard is another thing.

Jeff woke, washed and dressed, went into the kitchen to find Karen dressed and doing his breakfast. He was so engrossed in what papers he wanted to take with him he did not ask her about her day and what she was doing. He was being thoughtless like most men. When at times she pointed out how thoughtless he could be, he was mortified, as he would not hurt her for the world.

Karen was used to him being so engrossed in his endeavours. She knew a man with his principles needed space and time, and she loved him dearly.

Jeff hugged and kissed Karen goodbye, got in his car and drove to the mainland. The traffic was heavy and as he climbed the hill that overlooked the Estuary he could see across the view of the river and out to sea. The traffic stopped and Jeff was held in a queue whilst an altercation was sorted out by two irate drivers. From where he was stopped on the hill, Jeff could see right over the Estuary. He was puzzled to see a gas ship at the gas terminal and what looked like another gas ship coming into the estuary area.

As he puzzled over this, he had always understood that no gas ship should be in the same vicinity of another gas ship when one of them is doing a ship to shore unloading operation.

Jeff was brought out of his reverie when he heard the sound of car horns telling him the traffic had started moving. He drove up the hill to where there had been a slight accident between two cars that had blocked the traffic flow and causing the hold-up. The two drivers were exchanging insurance details. He drove passed where the two cars were on the side of the road, he then made his way onto the community center where he was due to meet Bob.

Bob was waiting for him as they met in the car park.

He welcomed him and said, "we had better hurry, I think they started earlier than expected", it was then Bob quietly slipped Jeff some papers and said to him "very quietly look at those later", they hurried inside the Community Center and joined the meeting.

As they went into the Center, they did not see they were being followed into the building by a man in a dark suit who was taking advantage of the shadows and watching them intently. The Center main meeting hall was ornately decorated and crowded with people attending the meeting. The meeting had just started and Bob asked Jeff to sit in the empty chair beside him. Jeff looked around at the ornate old building and its tapestries hanging from the wall and the medieval archways and alcoves. Jeff and Bob did not have the opportunity to speak to one another. The meeting droned on until there was a comfort break.

Jeff tried to mention about the papers Bob had given him but Bob quickly hushed him up with a warning look, then whispered, "look at them later in private", then added in a louder voice to cover-up their conversation, "you can help yourself to coffee, it is in the alcove over there".

Jeff got up and went to get himself a cup of coffee from the tray by the wall of one of the alcoves, he asked Bob if he wanted sugar in his, Bob nodded, then he turned and was watching someone on the other side of the meeting room very intently. It was at that moment that all of Jeff's world changed forever.

Suddenly Jeff felt the pressure wave of a massive concussion of an explosion that made the windows crash inwards and rocked the building, shaking it violently. The old building was not made to take the pressure of such a violent explosion and the building started to collapse, a large piece of masonry fell from the ceiling and crashed down onto where Bob and his group were sitting.

In the pressure wave of the blast, Jeff had been thrown off his feet and into the alcove by the blast. He hit his head against the wall violently and everything went black for a while.

He was covered by a cloud of dust and debris and sharp pieces of plaster and wood but luckily the shelter of the alcove saved him from the worst of the flying debris.

Dazed and with his head ringing and choking back the dust, he looked around him trying to make sense out of what had happened, the shifting cloud of dust settling around him and still hanging cloyingly in the air.

Jeff gazed somewhat dazedly at what had been the inside of a beautiful listed building with walls draped in large ornately coloured tapestries, old pictures, stained glass windows and plaques on the walls all of which were now torn, broken or totally destroyed and in pieces. It was so sad that this sort of damage had been done in an instant to something that looked as though it had lasted hundreds of years. Jeff's head had hurt badly, his mind was spinning trying to make sense of the situation, there was a concussive ringing in his ears. as the dust slowly cleared. His mind was reeling and his first thought was that it had been a terrorist bomb that had exploded nearby at the Central Command Building across the road to the hall.

What made him first think of terrorism was that before Jeff had retired and for most of his working life he had been involved in security. He had worked his way up to be the head of security of a major London bank and had been highly respected. He had been caught up in a bomb attack in London many years before and had been lucky to survive whilst others around him had died or been badly injured he had escaped with hardly a scratch, but the memory of that day had been ingrained on his mind and he would never forget it.

As the dust had started to settle and his head started to clear, Jeff had looked across to where he had been sitting prior to the explosion. He saw a large pile of masonry and rubble and the twisted and broken bodies of his friends, some he had just met. There was a pit of fear in his stomach as he realised he was just there a few seconds ago.

Jeff staggered over rubble to them, to see if he could help, but it was too late. He had frantically scrabbled through the debris to find Bob but his friend had been pinned under a large piece of concrete. Jeff cleared the dust from Bob's face. Bob had looked at him and whispered "Why?" and then the light had gone from his eyes.

As he stared down at Bob's dead body, all that was tumbling through Jeff's mind was what happened, and why? He was also coming to a strong opinion from one or two things that had happened in connection with Bob quite recently, also that Bob knew more than he was letting on, and his coat buttoned up over more than one layer, he thought Bob also knew more about issues than he was prepared to let on.

He had been going to ask Bob for his opinion on it after the meeting, but events had now overtaken the situation.

Dazed and confused as to what had happened, Jeff had glanced around him and at first perceived only an eerie silence, then, the ominous creaking of masonry crumbling and creaking wood. Glancing upwards he saw the top parts of the wall of the building begin to tilt inwards and go out of kilter.

A very large piece of broken masonry swayed inwards and came crashing down towards him. He dived for the safety of the alcove into which the initial blast had thrown him, just as the top part of the wall crashed down onto where he had been standing, a large lump of concrete flew through the air and caught Jeff a glancing blow to the side of his head, then everything black. He was buried under a covering of loose rubble and dust.

A throbbing pain that came pounding into his head had greeted him as he had slowly regained consciousness. How long he had been unconscious he did not know but guessed by glancing at the time on his watch that it could not have been more than a couple of hours. He had looked around to see the building in ruins.

The alcove where he had lain was covered in dust. The alcove had protected him from the collapse of the building, he could have been the only survivor from everyone in the building. Where Bob and his friends had died was a large pile of heavy rubble covered in dust, unbeknown to Jeff it had been the following day that he had come to, he staggered and scrambled out of the alcove like a grey monster covered in dust. He tried to brush himself down as best as he could.

Looking around at the ruination of what had once been a beautiful building, now with the tapestries in rags, and the building creaking ominously, he stumbled his way across the rubble and staggered out into the blinding daylight and onto the street.

As Jeff climbed from the ruins of the building he came out of his reverie and staggered into the arms of a soldier, the soldier said abruptly "You gave me a fright", then added, "that building has been searched already, I never expected to see anyone come out alive, let alone walking, is there any more survivors we missed?".

Jeff turned around shook his head and winced as it brought back the pain in his head and looked at the collapsed building he had just come from and could not believe he had survived its total collapse.

Jeff saw his car where he had parked it, it was now half-buried under a pile of rubble and broken masonry, the devastation that surrounded them both was like a scene from a war movie, some buildings were wrecked whilst others seem hardly touched.

The soldier asked him his name, he told him it was Jeff Baker, the soldier introduced himself, he also told Jeff it was John, and then added he had just come from his unit to report to his officer at Central Command hoping to hear of his promotion to Sergeant.

Then John the soldier looked at him and said, you look as though you've been dragged through a hedge backwards, then he saw the blood running from Jeff's wound so he told him of first aid units being erected near here to take care of any local casualties.

John added his girlfriend who is one of the nurses was working there, pointing down the street, he said, "the makeshift first-aid post is starting up over there you can't miss it, you'd better go and get yourself checked out, by the looks of it you have had a nasty bang on the head, then you better report to the Police station around the corner they might be able to help you".

The Soldier added, "what's left of my unit, is over there", He pointed to some smouldering ruins, "I must get to my mates, it looks like we have our work cut out", and then added as he walked off, "why is it always up to us squaddies? The politicians create the bloody problem and we have to pull them out of the shit when it all goes wrong". He then marched off looking bemused but determined.

Still bewildered, Jeff staggered to the makeshift first-aid unit that John had directed him to. A young nurse had spotted him and said, "Hey, you'd better come over here and let me clean you up. that looks like a bad cut you have there".

Considering the utter chaos that was all around them, it had seemed so surreal that he should be sitting having his head dressed and bandaged and talking to a young chatty nurse who was very sweet, she let him know her name was Mary. She told him she had been drafted in from the local hospital to set up this new first aid unit because she had a sister who lived nearby who she could stay with. As his head cleared, he asked her, if she knew what was going on? all she could tell him was, there had been a large explosion coming from the Estuary area and there were many casualties.

As she chatted, she told him she was sweet on the soldier who had sent him to the first aid unit. She had seemed so proud that he was due for promotion to sergeant quite soon.

As she had been finishing dressing his wound a medical officer came in and said, leave off doing minor injuries, as we have hundreds of seriously injured people coming in soon to see to, and minor injuries will have to wait. Operate a triage system from now on.

Mary had slipped him some pain killers for his headache and had said, "I must go, it looks as though we are going to be very busy. By the way, if you see John, please could you tell him I love him and to be careful, also I will be staying at my sister's and I will see him when I can".

Jeff thanked her and then had replied that if he saw her soldier boy John, he would pass on her regards and then he walked out of the makeshift first-aid post and what passed for civilization.

Feeling a bit more human, Jeff made his way down the road and came across a makeshift sign on a building saying "temporary police station". He climbed the steps to the building and went into a large reception room.

He was greeted with what seemed to be utter chaos. People were shouting loudly to be heard above the din of everyone shouting at once and demanding to know what had happened. Some women were in tears, some were pleading and begging to know about loved ones, some were angry and demanding to be told what had happened to their families and friends and what the authorities were prepared to do to sort things out, and find their missing relatives.

The desk sergeant finally stood on a chair, withdrew a whistle from his crumpled tunic pocket and blew on it loudly. The shrill noise had pierced right through Jeff's head, but it had also had the desired effect as everybody quietened down to listen to what the Sergeant had to say.

The sergeant said, "Don't ask me any details because I don't know any, all I know is there has been a very large explosion in the Estuary area and we have been informed that martial law will be imposed in that area whilst the emergency services do their job".

Jeff's heart had sunk, he immediately thought of Karen, hoping against hope she managed to survive, wishing he had not been so selfish about going to his meeting, he wanted to know more about the situation and the desk sergeant seemed to be the man to tell him.

He had edged his way towards the desk sergeant. The desk sergeant had looked at him and it seemed he recognised Jeff, then with a look of contempt, stated nonchalantly, it looks like you've been through the wars recently.

Jeff said, Sergeant, you said there has been a disaster in the Estuary area? the Sergeant looked directly at him, seemed to be weighing Jeff up, then asked, do have you have family there?

Jeff had nodded, then stated, I came from there this morning.

The Sergeant replied, I am so sorry, we are keeping a log where we can, and where any survivors are, before you say anything there are always survivors, so for the register, what is your name?

Jeff told him his name was Jeff Baker, the Sergeant's face stiffened and said very curtly, take a seat, and I will see what I can find out.

The Sergeant left his position behind the long desk and exited through another door behind him into what Jeff thought must be other offices or rooms.

After about 10 minutes the Sergeant had returned and very abruptly asked, him to follow him through into the office area.

Jeff had followed him into a room and the Sergeant told him to take a seat and, someone will have a word with you. The Sergeant was very abrupt surly and he left the room to return to the crowded front desk.

A few minutes later a well-dressed man in a pinstriped suit came through another door and promptly asked Jeff to confirm his name and address, Jeff complied.

The man was quite sinister and begun the interview by saying, You don't need to know my name, all you need to know is, I work for a Government department that you won't know exists, and it's lucky for you I was in the area.

The man then added, "The Sergeant recognised you from the television broadcast you were on last week, you were being interviewed about a high profile meeting you were supposed to be attending at the Meeting Hall in the Estuary area on environmental issues, The Sergeant has a daughter and her family who live in the Estuary area so he takes a close interest on what happens there".

The man then turned very surly saying, "Now what I want to know is why you are here? Why were you not at that meeting in the Estuary? Where the hell Bob is? And what did you do with his attaché case? You will tell me what you know and how you are involved in this explosion in the Estuary? Or you will go out of here in a pine box". He then continued shouting at Jeff and was getting a very sinister and a nasty attitude towards him, stating, "You people will go to any lengths to highlight your cause, but this is a step too far. Until I get some answers you will never see daylight".

Then paused again, and very menacingly said, "tell me what I want to know or I could let the Sergeant in for a while as he has a personal interest in this, his granddaughter is the apple of his eye".

Jeff was shocked at the turn of events that had happened so quickly ever since he entered the temporary Police Station.

He turned on the man, ready to go down fighting, "Whoa, pull your neck back in and let me answer for god's sake!" Jeff ordered angrily. "Draw yourself some breathe before you die of oxygen deprivation".

After a pause, and when the two men and finished eyeballing each other intently, like two circling gladiators, the man said, "Well what have you got to say?".

Jeff could not see a way out of his dilemma, he finally explained reluctantly what had happened up to date, how he had met Bob and how they were helping each other, and finished telling him how Bob had died in his arms in the collapsed building.

"Don't lie to me", the man retorted, "no-one managed to get out of that building alive, the man then scoffed. We made sure and searched it".

"I then took the Soldiers advice and came here to find out what's happened. And your sergeant put me in here.

I didn't know until 10 pm, last night, that the meeting had been changed by Bob from the Estuary to the Mainland", he said, "he had to meet someone very important here as soon as the meeting was over and rather than cancel, he asked if I could make the journey to here and he would be able to kill two birds with one stone, so is there anything else for your interrogation? or do you get the thumbscrews out now?" Jeff said, very belligerently.

Jeff now waited for the next move the man was going to do, to find out where he stood.

It suddenly became very quiet for a little while. Jeff's thoughts went back to what his friend Doug had said about him ending up in a slab of concrete propping up a motorway, knowing Doug had died in the police cells and no one was found guilty for his death.

Jeff's mind was doing overtime, in his befuddled state he was trying to get some sort of sense out of the situation, then things started to dawn on him, he thought to himself, how come this man knew about Bob, their meeting, and that Bob had had an attaché case?

Jeff suddenly had this wild idea and said out loud, "Can I ask, was that person Bob was meeting you?" The atmosphere in the room changed instantly.

"That is none of your business, keep your nose out of it", the man said dismissively.

Jeff had realised straight away that he had guessed right and that he had also touched a very raw nerve.

This puzzled Jeff, as he had believed that Bob was what he had seemed, but he had his suspicions that Bob's coat buttoned up over more than just one layer. Bob gave the impression he was a concerned environmentalist with legal knowledge who wanted to do something for the good of the community, not a spy for what was some sort of secret service with a hidden agenda.

"What do you know about the explosion? and how were you involved?" the man suddenly asked.

Jeff was becoming angry over the situation he was in. He felt he was on trial by some kangaroo court that wanted a scapegoat. He was tired, his head hurt, he was heartsick and he also wanted some answers.

"I know as much as you do about this explosion, that's nothing, and another thing if I am here how can I be involved?" Jeff snapped at the man, "I have family and friends in the Estuary area and I want to know what's happened to them. I've had a good friend die in my arms, I've nearly been crushed to death in the last few hours and I have lost contact with my wife and family."

Then defiantly Jeff said, "so have you got any more shit you want to throw at me? If so, do it now and get it over with, otherwise, find someone else I can talk to, they might have something intelligent to say. Then I can have a grown-up conversation, and try to make some sense out of this situation."

The man rose above the retort and said, "We have to know what happened because we might need to nuke the terrorist bastards who did this and you might be able to tell us who that will be".

"How would I know whether or not this was an act of terrorism?" Jeff retorted, then added, "in the past, I have been a victim in a London terrorist bombing and I don't want to repeat the pleasure, thank you very much",

Then in an exasperated tone of voice, Jeff said, "use your loaf, this amount of devastation is too big for it to be a terrorist bomb unless it's nuclear".

"What else could it have been other than a terrorist attack to create this sort of devastation?" the man replied.

"Have you thought it might be an industrial accident?" Jeff replied. The man had looked incredulous, "don't be a Pratt, the Government controls the industrial world, and they would not be allowed to be such idiots as to let something like that happen. Apart from that, there is Health & Safety that keeps an eye on things, and they would not let them get away with anything that would be that unsafe. So, I reckon this has to be terrorism and you will tell me what you know, or you will not see daylight for years".

"Oh please, use your loaf", Jeff had replied angrily, "a few years ago they had a near-miss at the gas terminal but that was covered up by your Whitehall mandarins in the so-called National Economic Interest, I tried to expose it then, but I got buried by the faceless Whitehall Wizards, and besides no terrorist group has the capability of making a non-nuclear bomb that would create this sort of devastation without you people knowing about it".

Jeff then added, "maybe the Americans have that sort of power at their fingertips but the last time I looked we were at peace with the United States".

The man had looked at him and raised an eyebrow but said nothing.

This had started Jeff thinking and thinking fast.

He was being held for a reason, and the reason was buried back in that large pile of masonry in Bob's briefcase and until he could convince this man that was the case, he was going nowhere, and it could get very painful. And the joke about him propping up some motorway started to seem very real.

'OK", Jeff had said as calm as he could, "let's assume hypothetically that you knew Bob, and you knew what he was doing. And the meeting was with you".

The man's face had stiffened, but he said nothing.

Jeff had continued, "Bob spoke to me of this very important meeting he had to go to. He didn't say who with, but only that what I was confirming in my investigations if it proved his suspicions right, it would open a can of worms. But he needed to confirm it with the paperwork he had, the results of my investigation, and this meeting he was having. All I know is that Bob seemed very concerned, and that was unusual for him because he was quite laid back and a change of venue at the last minute was not his style", Jeff added.

The man had stayed silent for a few minutes as though thinking then said, "What was the information you were bringing Bob?" And then he quickly added, "I'm not saying I knew Bob you understand, or that we were due to meet yesterday, but I must know what you both discussed."

Jeff thought, yesterday? He must have lain unconscious in that alcove for over 24 hours, no wonder he was feeling hungry.

Jeff eventually said, "this is going to be a long story. Can I have a cup of tea and something to eat as I have just realised I haven't eaten or drunk since yesterday morning?"

The man went to the door, called the Sergeant, then asked him to rustle up some tea and sandwiches, also to get someone to have another look for Bob's case in amongst the rubble near to where the meeting area had been inside the main hall.

The Sergeant had looked very surly at Jeff through the door.

"We might be barking up the wrong tree with this one Sergeant. I will let you know one way or another. If I'm wrong, as I promised our mum, I'll turn a blind eye and let you at him first, before he goes to the cells. I think the same way as you do about his kind", he affirmed to the Sergeant, as the latter went to get some tea and something to eat.

Jeff had not liked this generalization about himself. This was why he had respected Bob, as at least Bob had seemed to realise and respect what he stood for.

Jeff had snapped at the man, "Do you think I'm some sort of swampy, political agitator, or part of the great unwashed brigade that wants to create anarchy, just for anarchy's sake?"

"Well, aren't you?" The man replied, quite vehemently.

"No, I am not", Jeff replied trying to keep calm, "I, and I believe Bob, came to realise there was more to this campaign than meets the eye, he like me felt there was too much money involved."

The man had stiffened at this and inclined his head, as if listening, "carry on, I'm listening and don't forget I've checked up on you and your history. for example, I know you have made some very powerful enemies on your way."

Jeff Baker had led the people of the Estuary in a successful Campaign against the siting of two oil refineries in the Estuary area. He had successfully attacked the corporate image of the Oil Companies and the Authorities that had supported them.

Jeff had made a lot of enemies during this fight, also he badly bruised the ego of certain dignitaries through the media, but during this epic struggle, it was the only time in history that Oil Companies had been beaten.

At the ensuing public inquiries, he had taken on the Oil Refinery top Q.C. and he had made an enemy of him during the inquiry, that Q.C. is now a Judge.

The Oil Refinery fight was a massive David and Goliath peoples fight that had taken many years.

During this fight, Jeff had been instrumental in getting the present Health and Safety Executive formed and the two £400,000 reports into the Societal risk of siting too much high fire risk industry close to residential areas.

Jeff also managed to get Planning Law changed during this process.

The result of winning this campaign against the most powerful oil moguls by the community, the half-constructed American oil refinery was dismantled and scrapped, and the other proposed Italian oil refinery stopped completely resulting in massive financial losses for both global companies.

Jeff had made many enemies along the way especially in the oil industry, and quite a few councillors serving on the local council especially Councillor Randle.

He was a people's person first and foremost and felt very strongly that people came before profit and politics. He had earned the respect of the ordinary people the hard way, in the school of hard knocks.

Jeff wanted to highlight the issue of the dangers of L.N.G. so when his local Councillor who supported Jeff, chaired a bi-monthly meeting called an "area forum", he allowed Jeff to bring the matter up at one of these meetings.

Jeff did a presentation of what would have happened if that major spill of 163 liquid metric tons of L.P.G. had been a major spill of L.N.G. and not L.P.G.

The scenario of his presentation was cross-questioned by other councillors that attended especially Councillor Randle and the other councillors he had made enemies of.

When they asked the Fire Chief if the presentation facts and the scenario of a major disaster that Jeff presented was possible, the Fire Chief could not fault Jeff's presentation.

This worried some of the county councillors and they recommended the county council do an in-depth study and a scrutiny panel formed which Jeff gave evidence at. This was into the "Top Tier C.O.M.A.H. sites, (Control Of Managing Accidental Hazard) within the county. This study took 2 years to complete and recommended 6 major changes in their procedures and Emergency protocol.

The local Council on this occasion refused the planning application. The Gas company decided to appeal to the Secretary of State, and a date for a Public Inquiry was set.

Jeff was going to give evidence at this inquiry as a "Rule 6 third party". He spent weeks preparing his evidence for the Inquiry.

Three days before the date of the Inquiry was due to start, the gas terminal marketing company pulled out, and the financial backing was not going to happen. The gas terminal had no choice but to withdraw its application. Because the Gas Company withdrew its application, the Public inquiry was stopped, but in doing so the gas company had to pay financial compensation to the other parties because they had prepared all their documentation and presented it to the Secretary of State.

This included the local Council and Jeff's Group as he had gone in as a rule 6 third party. It would be the first time in the history of planning. Compensation would have to be paid legally to the pressure group opposing the application.

This did not go down well with the management of the Gas Company, as not only were they beaten by a pressure group, but they had to pay compensation to the group as well. Jeff had made another enemy.

They could calculate how much paper, ink, etc. The time and effort and hours they put into preparing the evidence was calculated in so many hours at an hourly rate. This part of the claim they would be donating to 4 local charities.

The legal wrangle went on for months. Jeff's pressure group's solicitor donated his charges to a local church, in the end, there was a required legal settlement, but it was like getting 50p out of their hand with a spanner.

The Gas Company like the previous two Oil Refinery Companies that Jeff had beaten wanted Jeff's head on a plate. He had cost them multi-millions in lost revenue, plus during the campaign, he had caused the Japanese bankers and shipping company to lose face in a publicity stunt.

Part of the campaign that Jeff led against the Gas Terminal they held a referendum of the community to gauge the feelings of the population of the reintroduction of L.N.G. within the community. This comprised of voting referendum slips where people put their name and address and posted them into sealed jars which would be counted later.

As head of Security of a Bank, Jeff knew the easiest way of getting into any building or compound is to "Tailgate" (follow someone into a building or area as they let the door close behind them).

There was a visiting cavalcade of cars bringing Japanese dignitaries to the Gas Terminal as the cars entered the site they had to stop and get out of the cars at security to show their passes.

Jeff walked in the site on the blindside, as the Japanese visitors got out of the car, Jeff approached them did not say a word, bowed to them, they bowed back, he presented them with voting slips and a voting jar bowed and left the site before the security gate closed. The Japanese visitors took the protest voting slips and jar and went onto the meeting with the management, and asked them what they were and what they had to do with the jar. When management had to explain what they were, the Japanese were embarrassed and lost face in front of the terminal management. It got Jeff a lot of publicity, but he had made another enemy.

The jar and voting slips were eventually left on Jeff's doorstep with a note saying terminal staff can vote from their own homes, not from the terminal.

Jeff did not endear himself to the Management of the gas terminal but he had won the fight, Jeff was now getting a reputation of taking on the big boys and winning that made him popular with the community but he was lining up his enemies all in a row and that row was getting longer.

It wasn't just the gas terminal that lost out, it was the Japanese Bank, and the Japanese Corporation as well.

A little while later at an adjacent site, there was an application to install a Bio-Diesel Plant within their terminal grounds. Jeff once again took up the gauntlet of war, he gave evidence at another scrutiny panel about the societal risk to the Estuary community explaining that tolerable risk did not mean acceptable risk. He pointed out the hazards involved of the process which involved Methanol and Ethanol and the potential hazardous effects to health also the flashpoints and the firefighting measures required, the danger to aquatic life if it entered the water supply. It also had a violent reaction to other chemicals involved with the process.

The Application was eventually refused, and Jeff had made another enemy to add to the list. What Jeff did not see was what was going on in the background and the Whitehall Mandarin's scheme building in the corridors of power. There was a very big power struggle, and internal political moves were being made to control the energy barons of the country and therefore put a stranglehold on the political parties ruling Parliament.

In an overnight move, the Terminal was bought out, lock stock and barrel, in a secret deal by Sir William Waites, the site was renamed, they determined the site came under Port status and therefore any change in the use of the site came under the Port Authority.

Under Port Authority status their applications to change the site to store and process L.N.G. was in the National Economic Financial Interest after a lot of support from the Whitehall Mandarins and support from certain local Mainland councillors they got approval to process L.N.G.

Jeff was convinced that the old pal's act played a major part in getting permission through, but he could not prove it.

Jeff felt very strongly that the danger posed, if there was a spill of LNG in liquid form there was no way known to man to stop that spill, with those low temperatures everything within the path of that spill would be freeze-dried in seconds, the liquid would boil and gas off to form an unconfined vapour cloud, that vapour cloud would go on expanding 620 times its volume from liquid to gas and form an unconfined vapour cloud when that unconfined vapour cloud found an ignition source it would set alight the Unconfined gas Cloud and it would burn hotter than burning petroleum.

The nature of the gas cloud would look like a large fog, there is no smell to L.N.G. a smell agent has to be added during the process.

But no one on the council was listening, the gas company got what they wanted, and the politicians got what they wanted, the people were being ignored again, and Jeff was branded a scaremonger. Jeff let there be known, that there are two types of explosion associated with an L.N.G. spill. One is a "Rapid Phase Transition" that is when L.N.G. is spilt on water, the molecules of L.N.G. want to expand 620 times instantly so they explode (it is like dropping an ice cube into boiling water).

The second is when the gas expands and reaches between 80% to 95% air to gas it will explode with the slightest spark.

Unfortunately, the Unconfined Gas Cloud could spread many miles before the gas was at the right mixture and an ignition source found by the escaping Unconfined gas cloud and everything within the boundaries of the escaping gas plus the heat sear from the ignition of that cloud would be affected by that explosion.

This particular terminal in the Estuary had a history of covering up incidents that might have led to a major incident or a worst-case the disaster of a total tank failure.

Lately, there was a shift in management under a global regime, which was of great concern to Jeff as to the accounting of responsibility of the industry. The people affected by an incident at any of these gas terminals were getting larger.

After Jeff's success in leading the Oil Refinery fight and he had thwarted the first attempt to reintroduce L.N.G. into the vicinity, even though he had failed to stop it this time, the community looked to him to help stop the expansion of the Methane

Terminal, and he was trying to see a way forward, but he was facing the power of the Whitehall Mandarins that was behind the expansion plans, and a certain group of local councillors led by Councillor Randle were opposing him.

The man in the police station brought him out of his reverie and said, "I know you've got a reputation as a successful environmental fighter. I can tell you that that didn't go down too well with my boss when I found that out."

"Who is your boss?" Jeff asked, curiously.

"I've told you that's none of your business, all you need to know is it's higher up the ladder than you think."

"I can think up some very tall ladders", Jeff retorted.

The man had ignored this remark, and continued, "tell me everything you know from the very beginning and don't leave anything out, even a small detail might help to throw some light on this incident, as I gather this situation seems to go back a long way."

The Sergeant, at that moment, returned with a plate of sandwiches and a mug of tea, put them on the table, and said, "I hope for your sake he's right about you, because if not your life won't be worth a plugged nickel."

"That's enough!" The man said, "if what I suspect is true, he might not be the villain of the piece."

The Sergeant looked surprised but said nothing.

"Leave us, I need to get to the bottom of this and I need his co-operation, he might not know it but he could be the key to all this."

The sergeant raised an eyebrow, said nothing, and left.

Jeff had felt relieved that he wasn't on a one-way ticket to the secret camp of no return, he had heard about once there, you were forgotten about and your existence denied.

"Right", the man said, "let's hear it from the beginning and don't leave anything out. I'll determine if it's of any consequence", and pushed the plate of sandwiches towards Jeff, and waited.

Jeff picked up a sandwich, realising how famished he was and bit into it. His mind went back to where it all started, before long he had cleared the plate and then was sipping his tea whilst the man waited patiently.

~ 0 ~

It had all started more years ago than he cared to remember, he had been so naive then. when he looked back, he mused that he hadn't even known how to form a committee let alone a pressure group in those days.

How many times could you say, I don't care if it's made of solid gold and built by the Red Cross before that was old news and was not printed. He would have to come up with different angles and different stories to keep people's interest and concerns in the cause, and the press publicising the plight of the local area.

He proceeded to speak to three other friends and neighbours and they decided they met at his bungalow that evening and discuss what could be done.

From that meeting of four people was formed one of the most successful non-violent, non-political environmental pressure groups called "Stop the Oil Refineries Group" which was to go on after 14 years of campaigning and stop two oil refineries being built, which was the first time in Europe oil companies had ever been beaten. (This fiction on fact story is covered in "The Big Boys do not win all the time" by the same author). Jeff had realised that violence solved nothing, and in actual fact lost your support, and you had to use the political party's framework for your cause and not let the political party take over your cause for their own ends. A very delicate balancing act, as political groups are for the most part very blinkered to their own political views and eye someone with a different political view from theirs as an enemy.

Jeff had realised that whilst there were people that went into politics on a grass root level and did a lot for the community, at the top echelon there were political statesmen.

In between these two levels, he felt very cynical that "politics" was as the word said "poly" is many, and "ticks" are parasites, therefore politicians could be described as "many parasites".

During those 14 years, there had been some highs and lows in the campaign and some highs and lows in his personal life which had hardened him.

One of those lows he nearly did not get through. This was when his first wife left him and went off with his friend and fellow campaigner and took his boys with her.

He had come very close to suicide at the time, it was 5 years before he came to terms with it. It had been very hard to carry on each day as he felt the loss and rejection had been total.

He had had to take the loss, the pain, and the rejection, even though it ripped him apart inside he still had to carry on his everyday way of life. It had been worse than any physical hurt he had ever experienced. It was a pain that only dulled with time and it had left him a bit cynical and slow to ever trust anybody again.

He could eventually forgive her for falling in love with his friend as this could happen. He could forgive his friend for falling in love with her because he had fallen in love with her and worshipped the ground she walked on. What he could not forget or forgive was the treachery that went on behind his back that had caused him to lose everything he had held so dear.

The treachery had gone against all the principles he lived by. For this reason, it stuck in his craw, it took time but he had to let it go eventually.

If he had not, it would have twisted and poisoned his way of life, and then the Devil's disciples would have won and the code that he lived and would die by, would have been destroyed, and at the end of the day that was all he had. He would often say during the Oil Refinery fight "God protect me from my friends, my enemies I know."

Because Jeff had lived through those dark tunnels in life, he understood the suffering and trauma some people went through in life, so he volunteered to become a Samaritan, the training was designed to be very self-examining, but he got through the training and was a Samaritan for 3 years.

After five lonely years of living on his own, Jeff met Karen at a party at his brother's house. She had two daughters, one who lived in Scotland and the other who lived in the Estuary. It must have been strange for Karen to accept Jeff going out at different times attending a call-out from the Sam's, but as she got to know Jeff better, she understood him more than anyone as to why he did it.

For Jeff finding Karen when he did, it was like finding a valuable diamond in the dustbin of life after going through a lot of rubbish and only finding a piece of glass.

The refinery fight was coming to a climax at the time. They had forced the oil refinery fight to a number of Public Inquiries with the help of their MP and support from his local councillors, they eventually held up the building of the refineries for so long that it became a non-viable financial project for the two oil companies and they had scrapped their projects, therefore the people were victorious.

It had been the first time in the history of Europe that oil companies had been beaten and Jeff had felt very proud that he had been a central part of something that had changed the course of planning history.

To Jeff, it had proved that if people bound themselves together like a bundle of twigs no matter how strong or powerful the companies were, they could never break the people, and the Big Boys did not win all the time, inevitably his enemies were mounting up, but Jeff was not in it for the popularity stakes. He felt very strongly that people came first.

============

"Well, what have you got to say about today?" the man shouted, bringing Jeff out of his reverie and back to the present day.

"Ok. Do you believe Bob knew more than he let on?" Jeff asked the man.

"Maybe", the man replied.

"Do you know that there were certain Whitehall mandarin's involved in the acquiring of permission to build gas and oil installations for their own profit, and they used their position to get the installations built, no matter what the danger posed to the community they were putting them in?" Jeff said forcefully.

"Have you run through the stupid forest and kissed every tree?" the man said, sarcastically.

Jeff said, "it's all about accountability, and trying to find out who is responsible if things go wrong. Let me explain what happens when the layman tries to get to the bottom of who is accountable."

The seemingly Three Ring Circus and all the Fairground rides the general public encounters when trying to get to the root of the responsibilities is astounding. In the event of anything happening to find who is responsible for any problems connected with LNG operations.

The Three Ringed Circus of the structure of the LNG Industry and the rather haphazard Government approach to LNG decision making, as there is not an overall structure plan or a safe siting policy, it spreads this responsibility very thin.

The Government does not have a "Safe Siting Policy" for LNG TOP TIER COMAH sites, neither has the County Council, the Health and Safety or local Council, and there is no national overall structure plan for the siting of LNG.

The Merry-go-round of the LNG Industry, as it is seen today, is structured internationally as a chain involving the participation of a large number of individuals, corporations and nations. The LNG ships are typically designed, built, financed, owned, chartered, registered and crewed by different groups and these groups are usually based in different countries.

The ships themselves are part of a large project which includes the exporting countries, the importing countries and a number of companies which arrange to build and operate the other facilities that require

Storage tanks, Terminals, Gasification plant, Road Tankers and so on.

The parties involved in all this are bound to each other by the Ringmaster called Profit which controls the Roustabouts of strong commercial ties and are thus responsible to one another for ensuring that each stage of the project goes through without any trouble like a slick Circus act of a Three Ringed Circus.

Not one of them, however, will take accountability or the responsibility for the project as a whole or worldwide.

The Three Ringed Circus continues with the Fairground rides, they now push you backwards and forwards from pillar to post on the Swings of accountability to avoid and push as much accountability or responsibility as possible to the other groups, government agencies, gas consumers and even the people that live near LNG tanks with the attitude "it's not me, it's him" we only want the profit for our shareholders.

Being there is no overall policy and no safe siting policy the responsibility gap of The Three Ringed Circus for the people continues with the Fairground rides of the merry-go-round and swings to the bumper cars, where you get bumped from pillar to post.

Health and Safety Executive will explain that they are concerned with issues involving workers health and general welfare, safety conditions and general hazards posed by LNG and similar facilities.

"A Code to Live or Die by"

If evaluating a specific hazard on a number of hazards involving the storing of LNG in the Estuary terminal, they will be referred to the company processing the product.

If evaluating the future import plans of L.N.G. they will be referred to The Department of Energy.

If evaluating the environmental impact of LNG facilities, they will be referred to The Department of the Environment.

If evaluating National security aspects of LNG they will refer to the Foreign Office.

If evaluating the information on the safety of shipping on the River or coast they will be referred to the Port Authorities.

If evaluating the potential fire hazard of a Terminal they will be referred to the Fire Service.

If evaluating about terrorism or Sabotage they will be referred to the Home Office.

The Bumper Car Ride continues bumping you from pillar to post.

When individuals or departments concerned at various stages of an LNG project are asked

Whether they are satisfied with the LNG operations?

Or are they safe enough?

Or what they can suggest to make them safer?

Or should they be where they are proposed?

Then you are put on the spinning Wurlitzer ride

The response is very revealing, and the Three Ring Circus continues.

With a High Wire balancing act of "Not my Job", I only do this bit up to there, and I don't do anymore.

They then call out all the Jugglers for Responsibility.

They juggle the responsibilities like hot potatoes hoping nothing will happen.

So, they play Pass the Parcel of responsibility along still hoping nothing happens.

But if it did, then The Magician appears who can negate the responsibility, or if proved that there was a responsibility then if anyone is killed then avoids the possible charges of corporate manslaughter.

Holding up compensation as long as possible is an old sleight of hand Magical trick pulled by smart Legal Eagles because the monies set aside for compensation settlement earns interest in the company's bank account so to reduce the cost of financial settlement it is held up for as long as possible. The Magician waves his magic wand for it all to shrink in size or to go away.

The problem is inherent with the structural design of the industry and no Government safe siting policy.

If there is no control of these vast systems, it is open to corruption on the highest level, some energy companies were so powerful, they already ruled small countries and that power was expanding.

The man said, "have you finished? If so, you can get off your soapbox now."

Jeff realized he was getting nowhere with this man, so he changed tack very quickly and said, "How far can I trust you?"

Then added, "I don't know your name, I don't know who you work for, all I can go on, is that Bob appeared to have trusted you, and I trusted Bob."

After a few moments of contemplation, the man had said, "Ok. my name is John and I work for an agency that does not exist, it only answers to the Prime Minister direct. It's an organisation that is set up for every Prime Minister, it's sworn to, and answers only to the current Prime Minister of the time.

The organisation was set up after a well-known past Prime Minister was phone bugged and spied on by unscrupulous Whitehall mandarins as you call them.

I am aware that Bob trusted you and by the way, the Sergeant really is my brother, and he has got a granddaughter, who is living in the Estuary, and he is concerned about her, does that help? Is that enough trust for now?

Now tell me all you know whilst we wait to see if my man, I sent can find Bob's attaché case and hopefully the important papers you spoke of that was in it?"

It remained silent for a while then John started to question him again about his involvement in environmental issues and why he got involved when others would have walked away.

Jeff replied, "I don't like bullies, and these companies have been trying to impose their Jackboot policies onto ordinary people who can't or don't have the information to fight back."

After a while, a man much resembling a weasel had put his head around the door, nodded to John, and said, "it's gone, and the body's been moved recently. It must have taken some effort to move that masonry to get to his case. By the way, we did find what we believe to be our friend here's the bag."

"I'll have that", John said.

`Christ! That was quick', Jeff had thought, unless they knew about the papers in Bob's case beforehand.

John said, "when you and Bob were spotted going into that building our people put two and two together, our man let us know, and he followed you in and never came out."

"He was probably crushed under all that masonry", Jeff said, "when the world fell in."

"The last time I looked, masonry did not carry a knife and put it into people's backs, also cut people's throats with it", the weasel-looking man said, very sarcastically.

Jeff looked astounded.

The weasel looking man then quickly threw Jeff a biscuit from the plate.

Jeff caught it one-handed.

"Are we having a food fight now", Jeff retorted.

"You're lucky you're right-handed our man was killed by a southpaw." The weasel looking man said then the man added, "Our man was stabbed in the back, and then his throat was cut by a left-hander, then was thrown into a corner, and by the looks of it by a professional, as clever as you think you are, even you can't do that. So, for my money, you're off the hook for now."

The weasel looking man then added, "but I reckon your life could be at risk now, big time, as it seems they were after you."

"What?", Jeff said, totally astounded.

Jeff knew he had made a lot of enemies during his environmental fights, but enemies that hated him so much they would put a professional hitman on to him was unbelievable.

"Thanks", John said to the man, "make a report and I'll see it later."

The man nodded and he left the room.

"What did he mean my life could be at risk now?"

John said, "you might not have realised it, but you have made a lot of very powerful enemies, because of being so well known, the publicity you created, tended to make you a bit of an untouchable, because the press and people would ask where you were, and questions would be asked if you suddenly went missing."

Then John quickly added, "but not now! at the moment your best way to stay alive is to stay dead, and you need to stay dead under that rubble until this is sorted out."

Jeff had felt a chill run down his spine, 'This is not real', he thought, 'it's like something out of a novel'.

"Now tell me what you know". John said seeing the fear and horror in Jeff's face, "perhaps we can get around this."

Then added, "tell me anything that Bob said that might be important. Any papers you know of that might help? I need to know so I can get to the bottom of the mystery of why my agent was murdered", John prompted.

Jeff could not believe what he was hearing, Murder, Spies, Government Secret Agents, what the hell was going on and how was he being drawn into all this intrigue.

It was then that Jeff had remembered the papers in his inside coat pocket, which Bob had asked him to look at, and he inadvertently slipped them into his inside pocket as he had got out of his car and was walking to the meeting hall with Bob.

"Are these of any help?" Jeff had asked pulling out the papers from his pocket.

John had glanced at the papers, noting that it was a list of names, dates, and numbers. Some of the names he had recognised others he did not know. All he did know was that the names were amongst the top echelon in the world of industry and politics.

"You got these from Bob?" John had asked.

"Yes, he gave them to me as he met me from my car, why?" Jeff replied.

"Have you looked at this list?" John asked.

"I was going to look at it as I went to get a cup of coffee at the meeting, that was when the world fell in on me, why, is it important?"

"Do you know anybody on this list?" John asked.

"There were two names I've heard of, plus another one of them I've met. Why?" Jeff had asked.

"It's only a list of who's who in the energy world. The question is, what was Bob doing with this list? Why was Bob giving you this list? And what relevance did it have to your meeting?"

"That's easy", Jeff had rejoined, "we were cross-checking my list of names of people I was suspicious about against a list of names he had of people he was not sure about."

"This is supposed to be a list of suspicious people? Huh! You're talking about the untouchables of this world", John scoffed.

"I know", Jeff interjected, "that's why we were cross-checking our lists to prove, or disprove that the risk to our community was at the moment from greedy speculators, and not from some foreign power, or terrorist group",

Jeff explained further what he had always suspected "look" he added, "imagine the hue and cry, if the people of this country suspected, or it was proved, that certain powerful people, manipulated the planning system for their own financial, or political ends."

Then add, "if there was a very big accident in the gas or oil industry that caused a lot of deaths?

the ramifications would be worldwide and it would totally destroy them and their global empire, but if it was proved that there had been a terrorist attack on these installations that killed hundreds of people, then that would be an act of war, and no blame would pass to the gas and oil moguls and their regime, and their global power would stay intact."

John had whistled, "you spin a good yarn, I'll give you that, can any of this be proved?"

"Well", Jeff replied cautiously, "in my bag is another list, and those two lists need matching up with the same people on both.

My list should work upwards in importance", Jeff said, "Bob's list should work downwards in importance, and if I'm right somewhere in the middle they should meet up at the same name or names, then the trail to the top person or persons involved gets exposed.

By putting the names on the list together, the lists tell a story, but apart they are just a list of people's names. Bob knew or knew of, most of the people on his list, unfortunately, I do not know who they are, or what they do. I only know the people on my own list, what, or who, they represent."

"Ok", said John, "if you are to be believed, let's marry up the two lists and see what we come up with."

John got both lists and put them on the table together, spreading them out to look at them.

After some time, John said, "See, nothing! On your list, there are names of some local councillors, county councillors, health and safety advisors and government researchers and Environmental Agency Officials. On Bob's list, there is the who's who of the gas and oil industry and some members of Parliament, two opposition Government ministers so nothing suspicious there, all you've got is a lot of red herrings and nothing more."

Then John's face suddenly changed, and he said, "Wait a minute. this man, Ray Wilson. Is on both lists, how come?"

"He's a henchman and a bodyguard to Sir William Waits, the President of UK United Gas. Sir William is on the list also, plus there is a direct link to at least two government ministers."

John mused "I met this Ray Wilson when he attended an annual meeting with the PM and the 'energy barons' as I call them, nasty little maggot. I know the PM didn't like him, or what was said by his boss "Sir William", they had quite strong words at the time. I thought he was trying to intimidate the PM at the time.

I was going to step in, but the PM said that he would deal with it", John volunteered.

"That's the link then", Jeff said excitedly, "I knew there was a link, and Bob's list could prove it."

John said, "If what you and Bob suspected is true, then this involves collusion between multi-billion-pound conglomerates and central and local planners, and it involves them right down to the grassroots planning. That is unbelievable!"

Jeff added, "If it was proved there was collusion during the planning stage, plus corners in safety were cut for the profit of "UK United Gas", then an accident resulting from those safety cuts, the whole pack of rotten cards would collapse, the top people and all their cronies would be held on corporate manslaughter charges."

Jeff added "it would be the biggest scandal ever. no wonder in the past they tried to put a "D" Notice on what I had to say, and brand me as some sort of anarchist or worse, all, so no-one in authority would listen to what we had to say, or what we could prove."

"If what you say is true, you're between the rock and the hard place", John mused.

Jeff replied, "I long ago stopped worrying about what people think of me, they will believe what they want to believe because they're not prepared to listen to the truth, and I'm not going to waste my life worrying or trying to tell people what to think of me as a person. I'm not important, the issue is."

"No!" John said, "I mean with all the media attention on this catastrophic event that's just happened, the attention the papers gave to you every week or so, will disappear and that makes you very vulnerable to these people."

"I've heard pigs fart before", Jeff, replied scornfully.

"Hey! Wake up, and smell the roses. I told you this Ray Wilson is a nasty little maggot" John said.

"Are you telling me I'm being threatened by you and this Sir William?" Jeff scoffed bravely, "when are you bringing on the goons to take me to a cell, kick me to death, and then my body disappears in an unmarked grave?"

John ignored this retort and said, "you're not being threatened by me, or the Prime Minister's team. In actual fact, the PM admires what you do privately but he can't say or even show it publicly. There is no threat to you by me or my team, certainly not after listening to what you have to say and what these papers from Bob prove."

"Are you actually telling me my life is in danger", Jeff asked.

"If Sir William or this maggot Ray Wilson thinks you're alive, with this sort of information, it could be", John replied.

Then John started thinking out loud, "for now, let's say you died under the rubble of that building, right in the middle of that meeting, and you did not wander in here, and we have not spoken", John mused, "where would you be safest? And where could you do the most good?"

"I'm not being a pawn in your political game of chess", Jeff snapped cutting the other man off.

"Face reality Jeff", John hissed, "these people play for keeps and so does Sir William. As I've said before, this Ray Wilson is a nasty kettle of fish and is capable of doing anything underhand. The last I heard they had some people in powerful places and you've probably come across one or two without realising it. You need to find a bolt hole to either hide in or do what you do best."

"Use the media to expose what you know to your advantage and become untouchable to the Wilsons of this world because they can't be seen to be involved.

There has to be a paper trail of some sort", John added, "They can't be this organised without it.

The second option will be the hardest, to get media attention now, with all this going on, and everybody being told it's terrorists. They would probably try to engineer it so you are in the frame as well", John retorted, "as I said, you are between the rock and the hard place."

Then John added, "until there is proof of some sort, like papers or information linking them all together, all there is are theories, and a few suppositions, all made up by anarchists, and trouble makers, to create instability in the country, and that's the smokescreen they will use to get away with their power struggle to control the country."

"Did I mention" added John, "In this political arena we are in at the moment, the PM is being attacked from all sides, and he is fighting for survival and his hands are tied and his power is being eroded by the likes of Sir William, who think the country should be run as one of their companies, and if people don't do as they say they should be, shall we say, sacked permanently."

"There are quite a lot of us who don't believe in a total right-wing society believe it or not." Jeff said.

"Yeah, Yeah", John retorted, "I know, poly is many, ticks are parasites, I heard you the first time"

John retorted, "and you don't do politics. But you could help to be the lynchpin in all this, if you wanted to be."

John added, "you could get to the heart of the matter and the people that seem to be behind all what you're trying to resolve", John remarked, "what do you think? do you really want to make a difference?"

Jeff said, "I have been making a difference for more years than you can remember, so don't tell me I need to do my bit. I'm not one of your raw recruits to be indoctrinated and manipulated to suit your purpose, then put back in the cupboard when finished with and denied they exist."

"Whoa! Whoa!" John said, "I'm not asking you to do anything, for all I care you can find whatever stone you crawled out from under and go back in there and pull the lid closed, but if these people find out you're alive outside the protection of your area where you are well known, they can make you disappear. Even in the Estuary, you won't be totally safe, not until the facts can be proved and this is resolved. And that's the reality of the situation."

John continued, "so, what's it to be, put you away in a cell for your own safety, and with some of the inmates they might be able to control and they get to you? that might not be too safe either. Or somehow get you to The Estuary without anybody knowing, see what you can find out, it is also where you can do the most good." "Now that is not going to be easy. Why can't you fly me in by helicopter or get me in by road?" Jeff asked.

"Have you had your brain removed?" John voiced sarcastically, "haven't you heard anything I've said? Everything is locked down. Even I can't protect you without compromising the Prime Minister at the moment, and hell will freeze over before that happens."

"Typical. So, you hang me out to dry?" Jeff retorted, "so much for all your fine words, and pontificating. What am I, another piece of cannon fodder for your political guns?"

"Come down from your high horse", John placated, "I didn't say I wouldn't help you. All I'm saying is that it won't be easy. At this moment, if it was discovered you were alive by certain parties, and you could point the finger even in a small way at them, your feet would not touch. At the moment, you're a loose cannon they can't control and a cannon that is capable with the right ammunition of bringing them down like a pack of cards."

"Look". John said, "at the moment only three people know you are not brown bread, and lying under a pile of rubble either here, or in the Estuary, that's me, my man you saw and my brother out there. It's not in my interest to say anything, and he won't say anything and they'll help cover your back if I ask them. Does that tell you where I stand?" John said.

Then John added, "at this moment in time, the only thing that stops you from being in the place of no return as you called it, is that you're more important to me alive, and as a loose cannon than being in a cell, and if what you and Bob suspected is true, I want to put these bastards away for a long time. And by the way, for the record, I liked Bob a lot too, and I want to find his and my other agent's killer."

John added, "it won't be long before all this area will be under military control, and our little friends control certain ministerial positions, that control the military, so they could be controlling the military without the military realising it and that worries me.

So, before everything locks down", John mused, "we need to try to put you back in the Estuary without drawing attention to you. If we can get you inside the cordon they are setting up to stop anybody going into or out of the area, you will be able to move around within the cordon and around the Estuary area reasonably freely, but, if we leave it any longer, everything locks down and nobody gets in until the area is sieved clean by them, so they're not implicated in any way. They will use this as a cover and say it's for a Government investigation, all to cover their own backs", John mused.

"Are you prepared to put your money where your mouth is? Or are you all talk?" John taunted, "I can't give you any guarantees, you still have a lot of respect in the Estuary area amongst the survivors", John added, "and before you say anything there are always survivors, you can move around better than anyone from the outside, and have more contacts than any plod trying to get information, so you have a much better chance than most of us getting the information to hang these bastards. What do you say?"

Jeff had thought about what had been said. he had liked the thought of the challenge, the chance to get even for himself and everyone, to prove that they had been right to oppose the siting of high fire risk industry close to any residential area, and it was all for the profit of the few, and not in the interest of the people.

"Ok, what backup do I get?" Jeff finally decided.

"At the moment, very little", John had replied apologetically, "no-one outside the cordon needs to know you are alive except my boss, my brother, and a few of my need to know trusted friends. We need to get you out of here this evening under cover of darkness.

But I understand there's a curfew due to be put on the streets from tonight", Jeff warned.

"No-one will question a police sergeant escorting someone after dark", John explained, and smiled wickedly, "he will take you to a house so you can wash up and get a change of clothing and be fed, then we'll see about getting you moved inside the cordon if that's OK with you" then added, "in the meantime, you get some rest, you're going to need it, you'll be travelling later tonight and we will get you as far as we can without compromising the situation."

Then John added, "We must get you inside the cordon before it's set up properly. They will set up the main roads first and then the back roads. Once they are set up no-one gets in or out without their names being checked and logged, a report being made on them and then put on the central computer, and that's when our nasty mates do their dirty work. They can find out your movements and track you down.

But if we can get you within the cordon before it's set up and it later tightens, you can move around within it, you can do what you need to do for a short time, without them knowing you are there.

"By then", John added, "I can try to stabilise what I can from outside here. So far, they haven't got the power to touch me yet, but if we don't do something soon, they could sterilize me completely and we don't want that, do we?" he added nastily.

John left Jeff to get some rest saying, "No-one will disturb you as no-one but we three know who you are and that you are here."

Jeff had lain back on the camp bed that he had been supplied with. His headache had eased to a dull ache, but it was still in a spin with regard to what had transpired in the last hour or so.

He thought to himself that unfortunately John, whoever he was, was right. There was a lot more to this than met the eye, and that people that were so-called friends he knew of if they survived, they were going to be very busy covering their own backs and hanging him out to dry to save themselves.

As Jeff had lain there, his mind had wandered back to some of the incidents that had transpired since he had been involved in this campaign when he proved he was right, they had patted Jeff on the back, especially when he stood and was counted and won the Oil Refinery Fight. But some were just as quick to turn against him if it suited them, some minor, some quite serious but they had all centred around a few well known public figures that had always seemed to benefit in some way or another either at the time or later when planning decisions were made or being made, but there was nothing that could be done now. It would be no use worrying until he could get there, and see for himself, and this gave him that opportunity.

He wondered how badly it had gone wrong and how and if his wife and family were safe. He missed them very much and remembered the time before he knew Karen when he was alone.

Jeff knew there was a massive difference between being lonely, and being alone. You can be alone in a crowd even with family and friends. Being totally alone is not a nice place to be.

With his mind doing somersaults he thought back to the time he had met his second wife after 5 long lonely years after his first wife had gone off with his best friend.

Oh, he had gone out and had relationships with many women that had been single or divorced during that time. He had never two-timed anybody, but he had not met that special person until then. He paralleled it to losing a very valuable diamond in a dustbin and having to search through a lot of rubbish until you found a diamond again, also realising you could easily get mistaken with a piece of shiny glass.

He felt he had found his diamond in life and he didn't want to lose it.

With his mind in a whirl, he realised he was very tired and so drifted into a deep and troubled sleep.

=================

He had awoken with a start when he was shaken awake.

"You could snore for England", the Sergeant said, "here's a cup of tea, drink that and then we can go."

"OK, I'm with you", Jeff had replied feeling a bit groggy, he took the chipped mug of steaming hot tea.

The first gulp burned the inside of his mouth and tongue but it also went some way to clearing the sloth from his head and bringing him back to reality. He also took a couple of the pain killers to get rid of the residue of the headache, he slowly came too and prepared himself mentally for another fight, this time it would be for his own survival.

The Sergeant had led him via the back door out onto the street. It was getting dark.

"We won't be seen this way", the Sergeant had said, "but keep quiet."

They had walked quietly a few blocks past damaged buildings, they came to a nice sheltered area with a quiet house nestled at the end of a terrace.

"Right, round the back and make it quick", the Sergeant said.

Jeff followed the Sergeant as they went round the back of the house and into a kitchen where a nicely rounded middle-aged lady greeted him in a friendly warm manner, "I'm Jane", she said, my Sergeant 'Dick' told me you would be coming"

'Her Sergeant and his name were Dick!' Jeff thought. Then said, "I'm sorry to put you and your husband to any sort of bother."

"Oh", Jane said, "we're not married. Dick's wife is in a nursing home, been there for years. He can't get a divorce, so we've had this arrangement ever since my husband died when he tried to stop a hit and run driver." She continued, "he was Dick's Inspector at the time."

Then she said, "They never found the driver or the car. Big green Jag it was, they say, all they could get was part of the number plate "W" something. They're still looking today but haven't seen hide or hair of it, but they'll keep looking until they find it", she said confidently.

Jane quietly studied Jeff for a few minutes, then said, "the water is hot for a bath if you want one and I've laid out some of my husband's old clothes. See if they fit. I've got dinner on, sausage toad all right? It will be on the table as soon as you freshen up."

Jeff thanked her, and said, "I do feel like a scruff bag, dirty and unkept, thank you."

As Jeff had sunk into the hot water of the bath, he could hear the murmuring of their voices. He felt the hot water gradually ease away his aches and pains.

He eventually came downstairs dressed in the clothes she had laid out, feeling all at once more alert and refreshed …. and clean.

"You look almost human", Dick had said with a wry smile.

"They appear to fit you quite well", Jane had said, "now sit down and eat you two. I've got a food parcel to make up for this young man", pointing at Jeff, "and Dick has some information to help you."

Jeff and Dick had started eating and remained silent and occupied until the plates were completely clean.

"Right", Dick had said, "Pushbike is the best way, and you can use the one in the shed. Tracks and country lanes are best without raising any suspicion, but we must leave before the curfew kicks in and the cordons are not fully in place. I can only go so far with you without raising suspicion and then you make your own way after that. There are a few things in the panniers of the bike you might need, if things get sticky, you never know."

Dick had added, "there's a mobile phone. If you find out anything about my granddaughter let me know, please. I've put the name and number on a pad in there as well as John's number. Don't let anyone see those numbers. It could make things difficult this end as this mobile phone is tuned in to a 10 to 15 frequency so it's not blocked by "COBRA" in an emergency situation like all other civilian mobile phones which have a frequency of 1 to 9."

Jane added, "I've put a flask of tea in the bag on the bike as well as some food, and some spare teabags that should keep you going for a while. There's also one of my husband's warm coats in the shed he used to use for gardening. I always said he was the smartest gardener in the street."

Jeff thanked her for the lovely meal and the clothes, and said, "I almost feel human again"

Jane said, "be safe."

Dick interjected, "we had better get going whilst we have the darkness."

They had made their way to the shed, got the bikes and made their way down the road without incident.

After a few miles, Dick said quietly, "This is where I leave you, you're on your own now so take care. I don't want to hear you've been picked up. Sorry, I gave you a rough time back there, but I didn't realise what you had been trying to do all these years. Like the rest I believed the propaganda put out about you, I know different now, no hard feelings?"

"No hard feelings", Jeff had replied, "I understand that you're concerned about your granddaughter, thanks for your help and I hope I can find enough information to put these bastards away for a very long time." They shook hands in the dark and Jeff made his way towards the Estuary and what was left of his home.

As the two main roads onto the Estuary converged at one roundabout, that was where a cordon had been set up ready for the curfew.

There was another little-used road which was an emergency road into the Estuary via the Creek barrier to the west of the Estuary.

This was the route Jeff took to avoid being stopped or seen from the hill that overlooked the Estuary and where the survivors' camp was growing in size.

He had only been stopped once and with the heavy bandage on his head he had pretended to be wandering lost and dazed.

He had been told to go to an emergency center along the road, it was in the same direction he was travelling, the sentry who stopped him was in a black military-type uniform. He was on duty near the gateway to a large house.

Little did Jeff know then, this large house was the central command post set up by Wilson, the professional killer, that was to hunt him and try to kill him at any costs.

When he got around the bend out of sight of the sentry, he went through a field to avoid the emergency center, and then on to the Creek barrier which was unguarded.

Jeff crossed the Creek barrier unchallenged, then he travelled on the deserted Estuary back roads to the north corner of the Estuary and an uncertain future.

~ 0 ~

Jeff got off the bike and pushed the bike and approached the north corner of the Estuary at a side Junction. A group of three men stepped out in front of him before he knew they were there.

"Right sunshine, who are you? And where are you off to on such a lovely night?" the man who looked like a scrum-half asked in a very surly manner, "and what have you got in there?" pointing to the panniers and looking expectant.

Jeff thought to himself, how stupid he had been to walk right into a trap, it seemed it was over before it began, but before he could answer the big bloke, one of the other men spoke up.

"Hang on a minute Dave", the man said as he looked closely at Jeff, and then said. "don't I know you?"

Then he looked at him more closely by shining a torch in Jeff's face and said, "You're Jeff Baker the bloke who was always banging on about the gas and oil people not caring about us people aren't you?"

"We heard you were dead." Big Dave said

"Take a look around you." The man interjected, "unfortunately, you were proved right about them not caring about us, it cost me everything I hold dear, my wife, and kid, his also", pointing to the other man, "and also Dave's wife."

"I don't know how my family is, or whether they've survived", Jeff replied.

They stood together, they seemed so united in their sorrow.

"Do you know what happened?" Jeff said, "some areas have been flattened, the further from the epicenter it looks as though they have hardly been touched, I'm terrified of what I am going to find at the schools."

"We were all together working away, all three of us when it happened. We came home as soon as we knew about it. We caught two looters by the public house. They won't be able to fix their teeth with broken fingers, or pick anything up for a long time will they Harry?" Dave said,

"That's why we're here now", Harry added, "making sure they or their friends don't come back."

"Now how come, you're coming into the Estuary at this time of night?"

Jeff trusted ordinary people far more than he trusted officials, he decided to come clean and take a chance on these local men, as they knew who he was, and what he had stood for, and they had him bang to rights, he could see there was no escape.

"I've seen you before", Jeff had replied pointing at the third man, "how far can I trust you three?"

The third man spoke up, "My name's Tom, this is Dave, pointing at the big man, and this is Harry. we've been friends since school. I went to a few of your public meetings about the dangers of putting this lot, pointing in the general area of where the installations were, next to us and you were right. As far as I'm concerned you can't do anything wrong. You can trust me and I vouch for these two. Why?"

Jeff had explained why he had come to the Estuary in secret, and what he was trying to do.

He also emphasised that if they ratted on him, not only would he not be able to find out what had really happened, but the culprits would be able to cover their tracks and get away with it, and nobody would be the wiser as to the truth of what happened.

"If I had heard this story a few days ago I would not have given you house room", said Harry, "but after this, you have my total support. If you can prove what you say is true, I'll help you bury the bastards, I never did believe that old bollocks about terrorists. They couldn't get that far up the Estuary without someone knowing about it", said Tom, then retorted, "that would mean they could get lost in a broom cupboard, and I'm certain our intelligence people are not that stupid."

He added, "how can we help?"

"I'd like to check up on my family to see if any of them are alive, but I can't be seen, not yet anyway. Also, I need a base to operate from, and trusted people to work with for starters", Jeff had replied.

"I'll check on your family? One of your boys went to school with my son, I can say I'm their uncle if anyone is nosey", said Harry.

"We can use the back of the Pub. It has a cellar we can get to and we won't be seen. People looking for family survivors go backwards and forwards from there all the time, so it won't raise suspicion if we come and go from there", said Dave.

"Good thinking Batman", retorted Tom with a wry smile getting into the spirit of the challenge, "that's probably the best place, plus we'll be able to recognise, or know who goes in or out of the area from there as well."

The big fellow Dave had turned to Jeff, coloured up and said, "I've not said this to many men, but thanks", and he held him in a big bear hug and spoke surprisingly softly, "you've given me something to hope and fight for, instead of hanging around useless. It also gives me a chance to help get the bastards who did this."

Jeff had thought, 'I'm glad I'm on his side. He could be a handful if you got on the wrong side of him on a dark night.'

"Let's get you bedded down in the cellars", Harry said, "that's what we've called what's left of the pub."

Dave said, "I'll stay here and keep watch. No-one will get past me, you can put your bike behind the bunker over there, it will be safe."

Harry and Tom had helped Jeff to the cellars. When they got there, they knocked on the beam by the door.

A pickaxe handle had come around the door frame followed by a gorilla of a man, "who's this?" the man asked of Harry and Tom.

"He's all right Derek", Harry said soothingly.

"As long as you say so", Derek had said, "you can't be too careful nowadays."

"We've taken over the cellars", Derek said looking at Jeff, "we swap the beer and spirits for food from the soldiers up the road. They like a drink and we can get some of their rations, straight swap like, you understand?"

He had looked at Jeff adding, "you know what I mean. We have to survive and it's up to us."

Derek then said, "Do you know they evacuated a lot of the surviving councillors and council officers from the Council offices almost straight away, so they would be safe from looters and mob rule? But as usual, we have to fend for ourselves. Bloody typical of politicians pull up the ladder Jack, I'm alright."

He carried on his tirade about the situation, adding "they really don't give a shit about the people they're supposed to represent. Oh, they'll bleat on, as to how come they survived, and it was a shame that quite a few of their colleagues and their families died trying to help the people, but they were in the bloody safety bunker in the council chamber doing an emergency drill, when it all kicked off, talk about them not digging in the same ditch as the rest of us."

Then he ranted on saying, "Oh! They have been on the news saying how terrible it was and how it should never ever happen again. But like you said it right at that public meeting that time, they could have stopped it. But they were too busy looking out for themselves, by going to all the bunfights put up by the gas and oil companies and only paying lip service to the people that elected them. You haven't seen a poor Councillor in the district since the gas companies got their planning permission. Elect them? …. I'd hang them if I had my way. They are as much use as a balsa wood anchor."

A woman had put her head around the door and said to Derek, "Derek, I've not heard you say more than ten words in one day and here you are on a soapbox, that's a first."

"Well they deserve to hang", Derek said angrily.

She had turned to Jeff and said nastily, "I know you? You're that Jeff Baker who stood up against all this and said it would happen. Well, you got proved right! Are you happy now?"

"Hey this isn't my fault", Jeff replied, "at least I tried to stop it, that's more than some did."

"I'm sorry", she immediately apologised, "I'm so angry and frustrated at what's happened. As you said, this could have been avoided, but they got on the gravy train and all lined their own pockets. I'm sorry, I shouldn't take it out on the one person, who tried to do something about it. My name's Jenny, Jen, to my friends and that does include you. Sorry again about my outburst, but I get so angry with all this greed that's gone on, and I do know you put a lot of dedication into trying to get the right things done, at least you tried to do something to stop them."

Jen was a medium built woman with a warm nature, she was a very friendly person, but there was a hidden hardness that had come with the school of hard knocks.

"You make a friend of Jen you got a friend for life. Even I don't upset Jen", Derek had said laughingly, then added, "she has a fearsome temper."

It had seemed so strange this big powerful gorilla of a man frightened of this woman's temper, but you could see he had a very soft spot for her.

"Come and get a cup of tea, not that there's much of that left", Jen ordered in a far more friendly manner.

"I'll have a look to see what's been packed in here", Jeff had said and reached inside the panniers of the bicycle that he had detached from the bike when he left it by the bunker on the back road to Estuary and brought with him and started sorting through them.

He found a large pack of teabags which Jane had put there. She thinks of everything, he thought as he gave them to Jen.

Jen said, "Hey, don't give us all your supplies, tea and coffee is the currency here now. Keep some in case you need them, but thanks for the offer", she said.

He gave her a big handful.

"Thanks", she said, "I'll be able to make them stretch a long way, the troops will be pleased we can have a decent cup of tea tonight."

As Jeff had put the rest of the teabags back into the pannier, at the bottom of the bag he felt something metal wrapped in a cloth. `I'll have a look at that later', he thought.

He picked up the panniers and followed Jen into the building that looked as if it had been shelled. "Did you say, Troops?" he directed the question at Jen's back.

"Well! you'd call them survivors that don't want to be away from their homes, or what's left of them. We all use this place as a center to meet and find out anything that's happening on and off of the Estuary. All we've seen is one helicopter and that flew over the gas terminal, looked as though they took some film and flew off. We've been left pretty much to fend for ourselves. What with the councillors being rescued and deserting us and one helicopter only looking out for the gas terminal, we have become the poor Cinderella that no-one cares about."

"This helicopter," Jeff queried, "did anybody see it land?"

"No," Jen said, then added, "Apparently, it tried to land on the Terminal Control Room roof. Mind you, it's the only part of the Terminal that stood up to the blast, so whatever is in there they couldn't get at it by air just yet or maybe they were having a good look round. They might have to come in by road and that's going to be difficult with all the debris on the road and the cordons being put in place.

Here!" Jen said, "I'm surprised you got here, how come they let you through the cordon at the Round-about?"

Jeff had answered casually, "I didn't come through the cordon at the round-about I came via the Creek to the north and back streets. They haven't set up roadblocks there yet unless they're locals they might not know of that route in or out."

Jeff's instincts told him he could trust Jen, so he continued, "it's better that I am honest with you as to why I'm here as well. Apart from finding out how my family is, and if any of them survived."

Jeff went on to tell her about his trying to find a connection between the Terminal, "UK United Gas" in the Estuary, certain councillors, and Sir William Waits.

He also told her, he believed that "if these people found out I was still alive, then these certain people would try to change that very quickly."

"Bastards", Jen had spat vehemently, "If what you say is true I'm glad you told me first, because I know who to trust and who not to trust, and if I tell them not to say anything they won't, not if they know what's good for them."

Jeff had felt glad he had confided in her. He felt that Jen was the salt of the earth and was one person to have in your corner when all hell broke loose.

In that case, Jen had said thinking on her feet, "You're my cousin who was staying with me and we were shopping in the Shopping Centre at the time when all this happened, and the people you met in the area so far will confirm that after I've had a word with them. You had better keep your first name, but you're too well known by your surname so use mine, its Jones. I'll put the word out to look for any activity at the Terminal and I'll get young Michael to find out about your family. If you let me have any details that would help, Michael can be very discreet when he wants to be."

"Now, get that tea down you and get some sleep, you're going to need it", she said, "you can kip over there in the corner, I'll see to it no-one disturbs you, and I guarantee you'll be safe all the time you're here."

Jeff had hunched down in the corner and drank his tea. He hadn't realized how tired and emotionally drained he was until he had sat down, and then everything had hit him all at once. His emotions washed over him and he found tears pouring down his face which he could not control.

It seemed that all the time he had been doing something positive his emotions had been held in check but now he had stopped and felt reasonably safe, he now had time to think of his own feelings. The dam broke and it all flooded in on him, he could not help himself. He was a ball of emotion.

Jeff felt an arm around him, and a voice saying, "let it out, come on, and let the hurt out", with his vision blurred by tears he could just make out the shape of Jen and he felt her strong arms around him.

"I'm sorry", he had said, "it's just everything hitting me all at once."

"I've been there and got the t-shirt", Jen had said, "so don't apologies. By the sound of it, you're the one person we have to protect."

Jeff had reached for the panniers and using them as a pillow he had laid himself down closed his eyes and immediately fell asleep exhausted.

~ *0* ~

Jeff had woken up, hearing a throbbing sound pounding in his head which gradually faded. He realized it came from outside so he got up to go outside to look.

Jen stood in the doorway and said, "It's not safe for you out there at the moment. That's the third helicopter this morning that's gone to the Terminal. That one landed inside, I hope they didn't catch Cyril", Jen said,

Jeff looked at Jen in a puzzled way.

She then looked at him and said, "Cyril and I go back a long way. We had a thing between us that didn't work out then, and he still holds a torch for me. He's the best professional tea leaf you will find. There isn't a lock he can't get passed, that's why he's nicknamed "the squirrel". He can squirrel his way anywhere." Then she added, "whatever is in that Terminal must be important because they've ignored people asking for help and only wanted to get to the Control Room of the place. Knowing the situation with you, I took the liberty and asked Cyril to have a look round, and find out why the Control Room is so important. He's due back any minute, have a cup of tea and some food rations we got from the soldiers while we sit and wait."

They had finished drinking their second cup of tea and were chatting quietly when there was a scuffling noise and a head popped around the corner and said, "Hi darling, it's all kicking off over there, who is this then? Is this the bloke you told me about?"

Jen had introduced Jeff to Cyril, Cyril was slightly built but looked very wiry and strong.

"So, you're what it's all about?" Cyril said with understanding.

Jen said, "come on, what did you find out?"

"Well", Cyril replied, "I got inside with no problem but whilst I was there a helicopter turned up and I had to hide behind an inspection panel when they came into the Control Room."

"You got into the control room without being seen?" Jeff asked, "that's unbelievable."

"That was easy!" Cyril said, "I could see through the grill of the panel at who was saying what to whom. There was a man called Ray Wilson having a go at a man he called David. It was about how stupid it had been to put the fireproof filing cabinets in the Control Room whilst the room outside was decorated and wanted the cabinets moved back into the adjoining room, left on their side, emptied and the papers inside them taken away off-site and burned as he didn't want any evidence found on site that could be linked with the new President of the United Kingdom.

When this David bloke said, he had no transport to move that amount of papers, this Ray bloke said, for him to go to County Councillor Rodger Randle's house on the mainland, where at the back of the rear garden in what looked like a big hump in the garden was an old large underground 2nd World War Anderson shelter that had been covered in soil and grassed over that was used as a garage. In there he would find a Jag covered by an old tarpaulin. He was to use Sir William's written authority which he gave him, use the car as transport, take all the files to the tip and burn them there, then burn the Jag.

Then this Dave said to Wilson why not take the papers outside and burn them?

This Wilson character seems to have more tricks than a clown's pocket, He said to this Dave bloke, are you a can short of a six-pack? If you burn the papers outside that will create smoke and you advertise, we are here, smoke from the tip will not raise any suspicions. He then added, must I remind you all, we are not supposed to be here? And if the Prime Minister or his cronies find out we are, we could all hang for treason.

When this Dave asked Ray Wilson wouldn't Councillor Randle mind me using his Jag, Wilson said, with an evil look in his eye to this Dave bloke, Councillor Randle was dead, then chillingly said, he must have had his neck broken defending his home against looters. I have to say, this Dave bloke looked terrified of this Ray Wilson", Cyril added, "I must say this Wilson character looks a cold evil bastard."

Cyril added, "I had to wait for them to leave before I could come out from behind the panel, is any of that of any use to you?"

"If what you say is true", Jeff said, "it's vital information that can link Wilson with Councillor Randle", and Jeff had tangled with Councillor Randle in public on more than one occasion over the siting of high fire risk industry so close to residential areas. One time, Councillor Randle had threatened him with a writ if he did not keep involving him in Jeff's remarks. Jeff had said at the time if I am not telling the truth to serve the writ.

Jeff had tangled with Councillor Randle on a number of occasions and made an enemy of him over many years, needless to say, they had clashed many times.

Jeff mulled this latest information over with Jen and Cyril, now we know Randle is linked to Wilson, Wilson is linked to Sir William Waits. Sir William Waits has powerful people in Whitehall, and he wants to bring down the Prime Minister and the Government so he can be President. It's incredulous. This treachery must be exposed, but to do so, he needed proof.

Jeff had to find the proof needed to confirm this, plus he had to get it exposed, both were not easy tasks.

Jeff had posed a question to Cyril, hoping Cyril was as good as Jen said he was, "could you get me any of these papers, or files so I can see what's in them?"

"Later maybe", Cyril said, "why is it so important?" Then added, "there was the other strange thing, why would they break the clocks and dials on the main panel, and alter the hands on them by what seemed a few minutes?"

"What?" Jeff snapped back quite stunned, "by how much time?"

"I could not see very clearly exactly how much they altered the time on the clocks, but they definitely altered the times on the clocks and dials, it was this Ray bloke who smashed the dials and altered the clock times by a few minutes. He also tore up the printouts from the machines. He didn't move any of the bodies which looked like they'd died because the heat had caused a lack of oxygen in the meeting room, but he took all their papers away with him."

'That was strange', thought Jeff, "there's more to this than meets the eye", he said out loud.

Jen butted in and told Cyril what was going on and who Jeff was and what Jeff was trying to prove. Cyril whistled and said, "The bastards! And they call me a tea leaf? At least I'm an honest tea leaf. I'll see what I can do." then getting into the swing of things added, "we need to stop these bastards", and then he slid out the door and was gone.

"Seems what you suspected is true", Jen said musingly.

"Yeah", Jeff said, "but don't forget these people are professionals, we can't underestimate them."

Jeff continued, "I underestimated them when I gave evidence at a scrutiny panel into the link between cancer clusters within a community and emissions and fallouts from flare stacks at refineries. This Scrutiny panel was ordered, and I gave evidence at, was at county hall, in part of my evidence I gave, I felt there were an exceptional amount of workers and their wives getting cancer, the wives because they washed the men's clothes, the men because the substance they were processing was very carcinogenic plus there was an exceptional amount of local people within the path of the venting of the flare stacks and the fall out of the carcinogenic properties within the substances being vented. If I had proved my theory, the litigation involving all of the oil industry would have been astronomical, but they stopped me using the specifics that I had on the number of deaths locally, they said I could only use general terms in the case I put to the panel. I was accused of scaremongering, I was accused of panicking the local people, and because of my well-known vendetta towards the local oil industry, I was treated as a hostile witness. The experts they put up against me were the big boys plus, they had directives from Whitehall to compare like districts, that had more cancer clusters than the Estuary area. I could not prove my case against the number of doctors they put up against me, and so the investigation was dropped, and I lost that fight, but you can't win them all."

It was then Jeff picked up on what Cyril had said about smashing the clocks on the instrument panel. "What I can't fathom is why smash the clocks and dials and alter the time?" Jeff had asked loudly. He turned to Jen and said, "if my suspicions are right, I need to look at the site from the sea wall, can I get there? Without me being seen?"

"You would have to be very careful", she said, "you can take Derek with you in case of trouble."

She called Derek and said, "go with him and make sure nothing happens to him."

Derek said, "you know I'd do anything for you Jen", the massive man said blushing, adding, "you can rely on me."

~ *0* ~

Jeff and Derek made their way slowly through the rubble and broken houses, with Derek in the lead as he knew the way better as this was the way he went fishing.

The scene for Jeff, was like he was back in his childhood during World War II when his playground had been a bombsite of destroyed houses and rubble-strewn bomb scared streets, it was strange how some houses and bungalows were flattened and others were standing, battered and bruised but still standing, all the windows were shattered, there was graphic sign's of heat sear that was caused by the Unconfined Vapour Cloud of Liquid Natural Gas, at those low temperatures would have freeze-dried everyone in its path. The cloud had drifted from the terminal on the prevailing wind and eventually found an ignition source, the exploding gas cloud had burned at a searing heat, those in its path would not have stood a chance, the area was smashed to bits like some angry giant had got fed up playing with its toys and had had a massive tantrum.

They headed towards the sea wall and devastation that was the remains of "The Smack" which was a 400-year-old public house.

When they had got to the sea wall the full extent of the damage the colossal exploding gas cloud that had wreaked havoc over the seaside of the Estuary could be seen, it was like something out of a disaster movie.

The surprising thing was that the sea wall was still intact though damaged in places with large chunks of concrete missing at the top of the wall it looked as though a giant had taken chunks out of the iron-grey stone.

There were scorch marks on the inside of the wall all the way along the area of the Terminal. Where the jetty had been there was twisted metal and pipes, the remains of a burned-out hulk of a large gas ship was at the end of the jetty.

The oil refinery up river still had pockets of flames scattered here and there within its devastated site.

The refineries across the river were still burning emitting acrid black smoke.

The gas terminal over the other side of the River Estuary looked as though it had been flattened as had the coastal installations on that side of the river. It was like a vista of an unbelievable scene, that was out of some sort of disaster movie.

In the middle of the river was the burned-out hulk of another gas ship and this drifted on its anchor chain like some large piece of flotsam floating aimlessly on the tide in the oily debris-laden water of the river.

Everything was either smoking or there were pockets of burning buildings all the way up and down the riverside as far as the eye could see.

As they made their way towards what was left of the Gas Terminal, it was like some biblical Armageddon that you couldn't comprehend, the extent of the loss of life and damage caused by this incident was so vast.

Derek suddenly said, "Get down someone's coming."

Jeff had to duck down behind the sea wall just as a man in a black uniform turned the corner and shouted "Hey you! This is off-limits, what are you doing here?"

Derek had reciprocated harshly, "What's it to you?"

The man realised the size and build of Derek and his tone changed instantly, "I have to keep everyone away from this site until the experts have investigated it", he had explained.

"I only wanted to find out if I could fish from here", Derek offered smoothly.

"Fish up the other end and not here", shouted the man pulling out a gun, clearly intimidated by Derek's size, "Now clear off!"

"Ok, no need to be nasty", Derek said.

The man snarled and levelled the gun then said, "you heard what I said, now clear off, or I'll shoot you and say you were looting to the officials and the police."

Derek had turned around and walked away back along the sea wall path towards what was left of the Smack Public House picking his way over the devastation that was once a thriving business.

Jeff had also walked towards the site of the Smack, but he walked on the seaward side of the wall so that he could not be seen by the security guard. When he was out of sight of the Terminal, he joined Derek.

Derek said, "Bumptious little bastard. That man and I are going to have a reckoning. He doesn't remember me, but I remember him. He was on a site in London I worked on, and he stole a lorry load of timber and tried to blame me and my crew. I'll do for him you mark my words, …. What are they trying to hide? I wonder."

"Let's look at the situation from here, what do you see?" Jeff asked Derek.

"A bloody mess caused by that ship out there blowing up and setting light to everything else, right?" Derek replied.

Jeff's mind had started doing overtime. He started to mull the situation over and was trying to make sense of it all.

Jeff mused, "what you don't hear, is the plaintive cry of the seagulls, you don't hear the sea lapping onto the shore due to the oily film covering the whole of the area, instead of the ozone of the sea, you smell the cloying smell of decay and death amid the devastation of what was once a vibrant community."

Jeff continued, "if that ship out there caused this, in my opinion, the burn marks from the explosion would be on the seaward side of the sea wall, correct?" Jeff suggested to Derek, "as you look at it from here, but you only get that stress and burn mark from the landward side and in the jetty area, the worst scorching is all along the landward side of the seawall right up to here. So, in my opinion, the explosion came from the Terminal and then went outwards, and what caused the Terminal to go up was probably an explosion during a ship to shore transfer at the jetty and the explosion that was started at the jetty created a domino effect that went right up and across the river."

Jeff continued, "if I am right, during the ship to shore transfer of Liquid Natural Gas or Methane which is the real name for the gas, a bursting disc might have failed as it did before, therefore releasing the Liquid Natural Gas, the liquid gas must have poured out the fractured bursting disc or pipeline and into the river causing a Rapid Phase Transition Explosion.

This happens when there is a spill of L.N.G. on water because gas is reduced 620 times at cryogenically low temperatures for transportation and storage in liquid form, the liquid gas is so cold, (below minus 270 F. or Minus 160C.) when the liquified gas comes in contact with water it expands from liquid to gas instantly thereby causing what is known as a Rapid

Phase Transition (RPT) explosion. It is like dropping an ice cube into boiling water the molecules want to expand so quickly they explode. This explosion would have set off a chain reaction of events.

It was a repeat of the incident that had happened a few years ago that had been covered up, but this time the escaping gas was L.N.G. instead of L.P.G.

The Rapid Phase Transition Explosion caused damage to the terminal, which in turn caused a total tank failure which is the worst-case scenario that has to be planned for, this created an Unconfined Vapour Cloud, which rapidly expanded in a cryogenically cold fog, freezing drying everything in its path.

When the expanding Unconfined Vapour Cloud found an ignition source the Unconfined Vapor Cloud Explosion and heat sear over 3 times hotter than burning petroleum, that ignited gas cloud caused the explosion of unbelievable proportions.

The explosion or something from the explosion at the terminal ruptured the hull of the gas ship which in turn released its cargo into the river that caused another RPT which instantly exploded. That explosion also ruptured and set off the tanks in the adjoining petrol storage depot. The ensuing conflagration from that spread to the gas ship in the river now in turn exploded. and that set off the domino chain reaction all the way across and up the river affecting all the gas and oil installations on the river."

To Derek's horror, what Jeff had been saying was a possible worst-case scenario that caused this accident and it was not caused by terrorism as put out by the company and the media. It stunned Derek, and he said, "How come you know all about this?"

"Unfortunately, I learned the hard way over years of studying my enemy, the substance they are processing, the lies they have told, and the lack of care they have to the community they are a part of, they are only interested in the profit they are making by cutting corners in safety, this was avoidable."

Jeff and Derek made their way back to the Cellars without incident. Jen was there and she asked if he had found what he wanted, Jeff replied, "Yes, but there is still a big puzzle to be unravelled."

Jeff mulled it over with Jen, explaining his theory as to what happened.

"So why go to all this trouble to hide it?" Jen asked, "Why smash the dials and clocks? Unless you don't want anyone to know what time factor was involved, or you wanted to alter the appearance of the time factor to make it look as though the ship in the river exploded first."

Jeff said, "What was that gas ship doing on the river at that spot when the regulations state there should not be another gas ship moving in that part of the river whilst another gas ship is unloading?"

He added, "That gas ship should not have been there unless they were trying to cut corners and do a quick turnaround on the jetty on the same tide. To save time and money, but that would be so stupid…."

Jen said, "that might give a good possible theory as to why they smashed the clocks and dials because of the time factor."

Jeff added, "If they are trying to say the gas ship on the river exploded first, it would show an earlier time on the broken dials and clocks onboard the gas ship then at the Terminal.

But if the Terminal exploded first, the dials and clocks at the Terminal would show an earlier time then the clocks onboard ship. It seems they couldn't get onto the ship and alter any dials or clocks so they tampered with the dials and clocks at the Terminal.

So, they wanted it to appear the terrorists on board the ship exploded the ship first causing the inferno, not the Terminal exploding first causing the conflagration. It would, therefore, leave them and the operators of the terminal blameless.

They also need a reason as to why the other gas ship was out there and what better way than to say they had no control over the ship as it had been hijacked by suicide terrorists but they had all died in the explosion.

If that theory is proved, firstly to safeguard the firm's reputation, secondly, to create political unrest thirdly bring down the government, and then to install a dictator. So, the story of terrorist is a red herring and a load of crap. This is a smokescreen to hide their profit and greed and use the situation to create political unrest throughout the country."

If this scenario of intrigue was right, Jeff came to the realisation, he was up to his neck in it.

It's well known that the Prime Minister favoured talking to terrorists first from a strong position to hear their points than having the dictatorial attitude that Sir William Waits has.

Sir William Waits' attitude is, if you don't agree with me, you're my enemy and need putting down, and putting down now.

Jeff was convinced, "Waits", wanted a dictatorship.

But he only wanted a dictator by the name of "Sir William Waits"

"No wonder they don't want anyone near that Terminal and want me dead. Proving any or all of this is not going to be easy", Jeff muttered.

On their arrival back, Cyril also joined them and had asked, "Did you find out what you wanted to find out?"

"I found out plenty", Jeff had replied, "this is bigger than all of us, but I can't let them win without going down fighting."

Then Jen interjected, "It's just been on the news. Sir William Waits has called for a vote of no conscience and the Prime Minister to resign for allowing the terrorist to be able to attack the U.K. and allowing the situation to get to this stage. Martial law should be declared and there should be retaliation for the high jacking of a gas ship that created the terrorist attack on the Estuary area straightaway."

"Well, he certainly didn't take his time trying to usurp the Prime Minister", Jeff had remarked.

"Can someone explain to me, why? This Isn't a terrorist attack?" Cyril asked.

"Not from what I found just looking at the area", Jeff had replied.

Jeff went on to explain his interpretation of what he saw to Cyril, also what it meant, and how he had felt that there was a cover-up going on.

Derek jumped in, saying, "That little shit down there. I'll do for him. No jumped-up little maggot is going to pull a gun on me and get away with it."

"He did what?" Jen asked.

"Don't worry", Derek said, to Jen, "I can crush little maggots like him with no problem."

"You try to be careful", Jen said, "I know you when you lose your temper, and I've lost enough loved ones without losing you."

On hearing this, Derek went red and suddenly looked very shy, but he had a beaming smile on his face.

"Do you know anyone with a camera?" Jeff asked, "as I need to get some photographs of what is down there whilst it's still in that state, and before they destroy the evidence", Jeff added.

"We'll find one from somewhere", Jen said.

'I picked up these when I went down to the terminal last time", Derek had said, holding out some little sealed units,"Are these any good?"

Jeff looked at them.

"Look, some are still working", said Derek, as he turned them over, "I found them near the pipes that came from the jetty."

Jeff hoped that these units were what he thought they were, the units were part of a device that monitored and recorded any dramatic change in pressure in a pipe and activated a shut-off valve.

Of the four units, two were still working. The other two looked as though they had never worked. Or if they did, it was a long time ago.

"There were also some pieces of triangular-shaped metal that were twisted at different angles", Derek added.

"Keep them somewhere safe", Jeff had said to Derek, "they could be important."

"Shall I throw the broken ones away?" Derek asked.

"No" Jeff had said, "the broken ones could be more important than the ones that are still working."

"How can something that's broken be more important than something that's not broken?" Derek asked Jeff.

"Because", Jeff added, "if it broke at the time of the explosion, experts can get the time of the explosion exactly, and probably the events that led to the explosion, and that could be an important factor."

"You can tell all that just from these little units?" Derek asked, turning one over in his massive hands.

"I can't, but an expert can", Jeff answered, "and if those triangular-shaped pieces are what I think they are that will prove what caused the accident, and I believe they could be the inner part of a bursting disc. A bursting disc is a device that is set to blow at a pressure just below the stress break factor of a tank or pipe, therefore, releasing the LNG before the whole tank or pipe breaks into the atmosphere at a controlled point."

Turning to Jen, Jeff asked "I know it's a lot to ask but can Cyril get some photographs of the inside of that control room? Pictures of dials, clocks, or get any papers or printouts that can tell us more of what happened? Ray Wilson and his cronies are trying to cover everything up very fast and soon there'll be nothing left to prove they caused this and it was not a terrorist attack."

"You don't think this was a terrorist attack, do you?" Jen had asked.

"I think it's more sinister than that", Jeff answered, "much more sinister."

"They wouldn't deliberately cover up an accident, would they?" asked Jen disbelievingly, "what on earth for?"

"It's a long story but I believe it to be true", Jeff had replied.

"We've got time until Michael gets here, and the kettle's on", said Jen, "Derek will keep an eye out."

"Well", Jeff began, "it all started when I got involved, at the time. "UK United" applied for planning permission to store and process Liquid Natural Gas (LNG) at the terminal. I already had this reputation for fighting the energy companies, as I had been involved in the oil refinery fight on a few years back."

"Involved? Is that how you describe it? From what I remember you were the lynchpin in that fight", Jen interrupted.

"Hey! I was only part of a great organisation, not the mainstay", Jeff had retorted.

"You never did take the praise for what you did", Jen had said, "I remember the exact words that Inspector at that public inquiry said after you gave your evidence. If nothing else comes out of that inquiry the people of the area owed you a debt that could not be repaid."

"Everybody knows it was you and not the councillors that stopped them from building their oil refineries", Jen added, "didn't Councillor Randle and certain councillors only stepped in and tried to take all the credit after you had won? Up until then, they were in the oil companies' pockets. Mind you it was just as there was an election coming up. Didn't some of them go to America with their families to look at a working refinery for 10 days, all expenses paid?" She said contemptuously, "and then they came back and said how wonderful it was that foreign oil companies wanted to invest in the community. If they wanted to see a working oil refinery, they could have gone across the creek to see a working refinery at no cost at all. But they said at the time it was a fact finding tour that had to be done." Jen said.

"I wouldn't trust them as far as the end of my nose", Jen added scornfully, "no matter what party they stand for, they're only in it for their own ends."

"Sorry", Jen checked herself, "I stopped you telling me this theory, but they do annoy me when they treat the people as though they're thick and stupid." She looked at him and said, "O.K. I'll try to keep quiet whilst you talk."

"I think it's a matter of profit and corruption over ordinary people and the people paying the price with their lives if things go badly wrong and nobody is answerable", Jeff continued, "this is a big gravy train and they all want to get on it, and when I say big, I mean really big."

Jeff continued, "it's a multi-national organisation with interlinked chains of profit that can in some cases control and rule countries. The energy source we are dealing with is Liquid Natural Gas (LNG) or liquid methane. It's stored and transported in liquid form because if you freeze down the gas to below a temperature of minus 270 degrees F you can reduce the gas 620 times its volume to a liquid form, therefore being able to store more, transport more, and therefore make a bigger profit.

The profits from this process are massive, verses a relative, small outlay. The only downside is if there is a large spill of this LNG, the consequences for that scenario for the surrounding area are devastating."

"How is that?" Jen asked.

"I'll get to that", Jeff said and continued.

"The Terminal had 250 thousand tons of LNG stored at the terminal as well as Liquid Petroleum Gas (LPG) and they wanted to increase the storage capacity to 750,000 tons of LNG for what they said was in the "national economic interest" of the country as a whole. As I said before, in freezing down the gas to below 270 F, LNG is concentrated down 620 times its size from gas to liquid therefore you can store more of it cheaply. The problems arise if there is a large accidental or deliberate spill of LNG. There is no known way to contain a large LNG spill. There is no known way to prevent that spill from forming an Unconfined Vapour Cloud spreading out at an alarming rate for many miles. The gas has no odour, at temperatures of below minus 160 C. It will look like a cold fog hugging the ground freeze-drying everything in its path, then as the gas cloud expands it rises and drifts on the wind travelling many miles before it can disperse into the atmosphere.

It expands three times faster on water than on land. For every bucket load of liquid, it will turn into 620 bucket loads of gas.

There is no known way to prevent an Unconfined Vapour Cloud spreading, if before it disperses the cloud finds an ignition source it will explode, causing an explosion with fire temperature 300 degrees hotter then burning petrol ensuing from the gas cloud if it finds that ignition source. The heat sear from that burning gas would reach even further taking all the oxygen out of the air to feed the fireball of burning gas.

You cannot evacuate the surrounding area in time because the chain reaction is so fast from spill to ignition.

There can be two types of explosions with this stuff.

One is known as a Rapid Phase Transition. This is when the liquid spills on water, it expands so fast to a gaseous state because of the sudden change in temperature that it explodes (it's like the same reaction you would get if you dropped an ice cube into boiling water, the ice cube would shatter).

The second explosion is when the gas mixes with air to a mixture between 5% to 15% gas and 85% to 95% air. It can be ignited by a slight spark. It will be determined how many miles the gas cloud spreads before ignition to the amount of damage that will be done.

Logistically, they can't evacuate the area in half a day let alone a few minutes it takes from spill to ignition. So, everyone within the vicinity of these installations is cannon fodder to their greed and profit if something goes wrong.

That's why we have always said this stuff should be located away from residential areas. We understand the only reason they want to site it in the area is because there is deep sea access for shipping and their biggest market is in the southeast of the country."

"Complicated," said Jen "but now I understand it more than I did. But you said it was not terrorists that caused this, how do you know?"

"Well, there was no mention of terrorist activity anywhere near here until after the explosion", Jeff had explained, "and if they had hijacked a gas ship, everyone would have known about it.

It was only brought to the Government's attention by a UK United source that the gas ship that was drifting in the Estuary had been high jacked by terrorists and blown up and that caused the disaster.

Sir William soon after that demanded the resignation of the Government and that marshal law be put in place until the terrorists were brought to heel stating this as a failure of the government to stop this so-called high jack.

I believe Sir William is using this as a way to get control of the country and put it and the people under his dictatorship."

"Perhaps I'm being thick", Jen said, "but you've not explained to me why you think it was not terrorists and if not, what caused all this and why?"

"Those sealed units and bits from a bursting disc that Derek found, maybe a clue to what happened", Jeff said, "I believe those sealed units and the bursting disc were attached to the pipeline valves.

The bursting discs are designed to blow just below the fracture stress point of the pipework, In the event of a fracture of the pipeline, the units operate a shut-off valve that is supposed to operate instantly and shut off in the event of pipeline failure.

These units and valves, as well as other high-level alarms in tanks, have to be maintained on a frequent basis, failure to do so can result in heavy fines or even shutting down of the Terminal.

The trouble for the operators is that to maintain or replace these units takes operating downtime and sections have to be closed and that eats into their profits.

With the breaking of the bursting discs or in this case the pipeline, those sealed units should have operated and shut the pipeline down therefore isolating the section of the break.

But if those units failed the pipeline would have been exposed to catastrophic failure which would have meant the LNG would have been released from the pipeline in a massive amount.

That sudden release of LNG onto water would have caused a "Rapid Phase Transition" (RPT) explosion which in turn would have set off a chain of events.

That chain of events could have been the RPT explosion damaging the integrity of the hull of the gas ship unloading its cargo which in turn vented part of its cargo that in turn exploded destroying the rest of the gas ship that was unloading its cargo at the terminal.

The knock-on effect of this was that the gas terminal pipeline was then the centre of the explosion and this, in turn, damaged the gas tanks on site.

You then had the on-site gas tanks totally fail.

In turn, this caused another Unconfined Vapour Cloud Explosion at the site which in turn damaged the gas ship in the river. The tanks on this ship failed, causing a "Rapid Phase Transition" explosion which in turn destroyed the gas ship and because it was near the other terminal on the other side of the river the concussion damaged the tanks at that installation and they ignited.

This, in turn, created a "domino effect" of explosions all the way across the river estuary mouth and all the way up the river. taking this part of the country back to the dark ages with this apocalyptic disaster.

This is all because of cutting corners on inspections and safety precautions to save time and money.

If "Sir William" and "UK United" can convince the country the accident was caused by terrorists and not by them cutting corners for profit they're off the hook and "Sir William" can try to use the chaos as a smokescreen to take over this country and install himself as a dictator".

"Proving that is not going to be easy at all", Jen said worriedly.

"But if we can expose them for what they are, then Sir William and UK United will have to answer to the country and the surviving families of all the thousands of people that have been killed", Jeff explained and then said, "getting back to some semblance of order will take some time.

If you remember, it took three to four years before the families affected by the Buncefield incident could get back into their homes and businesses but the companies that caused the problem were up and running and making a profit in a matter of months."

~0~

At that moment, a man about thirty-five, of stocky build, popped his head around the door and said "Jen, I got your message. I started checking up on …." He stopped in mid-sentence when he saw Jeff, "Who's this?"

"This is the man whose family you have been trying to find out about", Jen answered.

She then caught sight of the bruises on the side of his face, "who did this?" she asked.

"They wanted information about him, pointing at Jeff", pretty badly.

"The suits at the cordon", Michael replied.

"Tell us what happened." Then she added, "get over here and I'll put a cold compress on your bruises."

"Oh, don't fuss, woman", Michael said, raising a hand as if to ward off an irritating fly, "I've had a lot worse."

"Well, tell us what happened then", Jen insisted.

"Well", he said, "I got jumped by these three blokes when I was checking his bungalow. Apparently, I disturbed them checking through his computer files. They said even though the computer was badly damaged they could still retrieve a lot of the data and take it away.

They took me to a hall in back of the Half Penny Pub on the mainland, then questioned me as to why I was there?" Then pointing to Jeff "then they asked me, how did I know you? And did I know if you were alive if so of your whereabouts? They were about as bright as Alaska in December.

As you can see, they tried to be very persuasive, but as you know I've had worse in the ring. They let me go on the proviso that if I heard anything, I would let them know."

He had turned to Jeff and said, "these suits must want you pretty badly."

"Was my wife there?" Jeff had asked.

"Sorry, no. They asked me about that, and if I knew where she was?"

"Did you tell him anything?" Jeff asked.

"What do you take me for?" Michael snapped, obviously much offended by the question.

"Neutral corner you", Jen had said to Michael, "we all have a lot to lose in this. Let's not clash over others otherwise, they succeed and divide and rule."

"I'm sorry", Jeff had apologised, "I was ungrateful and I apologise for my outburst."

"If I was in your boots," Michael said, "I'd probably do the same. No hard feelings" and he leaned across and shook Jeff's hand.

Jeff had been surprised at the powerful grip Michael had for such a stocky built man, "look, I'm sorry about your wife and family", Michael announced, "like everyone else they didn't stand a chance, freeze-dried first and then incinerated. These terrorists are going to pay big time."

"What if I told you it wasn't terrorists", Jeff said to Michael.

"What?" Michael looked surprised.

"What if I told you this was an industrial accident that could have been prevented, but greed and political machinations are being manipulated to hide the facts, to create a political coup, and the people you met are the henchmen of Sir William Waits who wants to be the dictator of this country at any costs.

What if I told you we could prove, all of this death and destruction massive loss of life and total devastation was down to them, just so they can take over this country in a coup for their own dictatorship."

"They would want you dead yesterday", Michael said, "plus, try to persuade people nicely or otherwise to help find you if you were alive. But from what I gathered from them you were at a meeting in the Estuary at the time and didn't survive." Michael added, "so how did you survive, no-one lived when that meeting place caught it, well that's where the meeting was advertised for, wasn't it?"

"I wasn't at that meeting. The meeting I went to was changed at the last minute to the mainland, even then the building we were in took a hammering and a lot of people died in it, I was very lucky."

"That was lucky for you", Michael said, "but if what you say is true, they want you dead, big time, so you can't nail them for this."

"I asked around for Jen's sake", Michael added, "just because she asked me to, but now I know this is maybe because of them. I'm right behind you, and so will all the other survivors be", he reached across and shook Jeff's hand and added, "How can I be of help? You have my total support."

"I need people to be my eyes and ears out there until I get enough information to go to my press contacts to expose this, and get the takeover stopped", Jeff said.

"According to the latest news, the Middle East is up in arms about these terrorist accusations and are threatening a Holy war", Michael said.

"When you're out and about, see if you can also find anything out about the family Smith who lived in No 5 by the turning next to the Town Centre. Man, woman, little girl. If you find anything let me know", Jeff asked.

"Are they family or friends?" Michael asked.

"Neither, but I would like to know if you can find anything out about them", Jeff answered thinking of John's brother, the Police Sargent who helped him get back into the Estuary.

Just then Cyril came in.

"Hi, all, you want some snaps taken then?" he said to Jeff.

"Yes please, but be careful, these bastards don't take no prisoners", Jeff had replied.

"Right, what do you want?"

"Photograph's of the smashed dials and clock in the control room, any papers from that meeting room, get any shots of the jetty, the sea wall, and the drifting tanker", Jeff added, "but above all don't get caught. There have been enough people killed already and I don't want you on that list."

Cyril left with a wry smile.

"I will check on that address", Michael added and he then ducked back out of the door also.

~0~

After Cyril and Michael left, Jen sat down beside Jeff and said, "The damage is pretty bad across the Estuary and there have been a lot of people killed. If this is an Industrial accident being covered up, I will never forgive them for all those poor children in the schools that were killed. Those poor mites didn't stand a chance without an evacuation plan, but the authorities didn't care enough to do something about it. It's all too late now, thousands of people are dead."

Jeff retorted, "I wonder how they'll justify the decision to pass that particular planning application? Eh! They'll probably come out with some bullshit about it was in the 'National Economic Interest', or they didn't know or, they weren't given the full information, anything to do a 'Pontius Pilate' and wash their hands of the whole thing."

Jen said, "Did you want to look around? It's not a pretty sight. They haven't been here to the Estuary area yet to help us, they've been too busy evacuating councillors, dignitaries and their families from here, and the outlying areas, I hear they are putting them up in luxurious hotels so they don't have to worry about us".

Jeff said reluctantly, "Yes. Even just to be a witness to what has happened, but we must be very careful I am still a wanted man and anyone with me will suffer the same fate if we are caught."

They went out and walked across the devastated area and on the towards the center of what was once a vibrant community. They picked their way over the rubble of broken homes, windows were smashed and walls were on the edge of toppling down, scaring off the heat sear was like a dirty stain on the outside rendering of some of the homes, on coming to an infant and junior school, even though Jeff steeled himself, he was not prepared for the horror of what he saw. It would be seared into his memory forever.

Jeff entered the school gates, he crossed the eerie empty playground. He could see into the collapsed school building, there were parts of the roof lying at a drunkenly awkward angle, the windows and doors looked as though a giant hand had angrily smashed them, the paint was blistered and blackened, and there was the cloying stench of burned flesh and death.

Jeff told Jen to stay, and go no further into the horrific scene he was heading, he forced himself to approach the building with a morbid dread, trying to steel himself for what he was going to see and what he was about to witness.

But nothing prepared him for the horror that was there, only his anger of what happened to the innocent children drove him on, as he felt someone had to be a witness to this nightmare. As much as his stomach lurched, he hardened himself to what he might witness.

Jeff felt his stomach start to reject what was in it, as he looked around at the twisted burned shrivelled bodies, they looked like sausages that had been thrown in a frying pan and the skin had split and seared in the heat, the little bloated bodies were huddled together, at one point a teacher had tried to protect some of them with her body but to no avail, the heat of the igniting gas had done its damage. Everyone had been freeze-dried with the cold gas and then incinerated when it exploded. No one in the school had stood a chance.

His eyes were looking at something his brain did not want to know, but it was telling him that it was obvious something like the worst-case scenario he had always said would happen, had happened, and it caused this total devastation, the horror of this massive loss of innocent lives, would be seared into his brain forever, and no matter how much he tried it would never go away.

Everything inside the building was blackened and scorched, it was then the wind direction changed and the smell of death hit him. He immediately gagged and threw up, he staggered out of the building retching. What he had just witnessed would be ingrained on his memory forever, and he would never forget that smell as long as he lived.

He was glad he had insisted to Jen that he look in the school on his own, he did not want her to see what he had seen. When she saw him come out of the building and how it had affected him, she asked in a tremulous voice, "Is it that bad?"

"My God yes, worse than your worst nightmare", Jeff said, in a voice that was hoarse and shook with emotion and added, "you're never going in there. It is too horrible, but I swear by the code I live by, I will make them pay for this, or I will die trying."

They carried on walking towards the cellars, as they passed what was a grocer's shop, the basement was open, Jen slipped in to pick up some tins of food, as she went into the building Jeff heard the throbbing sound of the rotors of a helicopter approaching them, Jeff dived for cover, hoping he had not been seen, the helicopter circled once, and then flew on to the gas terminal building.

Jeff called out to Jen, "We'd better get going before the helicopter comes back."

They had just got back to the Cellars when they heard the throbbing of the helicopter engine again, this time it circled the area where they had been, it looked as though it landed for a few minutes, then took off again, circled around and flew off.

"That was close", Jen said quite relieved, "We'll have to be more careful, if they had caught you, it would all be over for all of us."

They had sat talking about what Jeff had seen at the school for some time over a cup of tea, it seemed talking about it helped ease the nightmare. Jen could see the effect it had on Jeff, the more he talked about it, the more determined he was getting to find the evidence to put the people who had played any part in this away for keeps.

As it started to get dark, they heard a scraping sound outside, they were suddenly alert.

They went out to investigate and found Cyril scrabbling into the doorway with blood running down his chest and arm, "Bastard got me", he had gasped.

"What happened?" Jeff asked.

"Got what you wanted", Cyril said, "but the bastard saw me. Must be slipping in my old age" he grimaced, "mind you he only saw me after I'd been inside and was making my way back."

"Who saw you?" Jeff asked.

"The bloke in the helicopter, he had Wilson with him", Cyril said, "as he landed there, I took a photo of him and that's when he chased me. He told me to stop and hand over the camera or he would shoot to kill.

I didn't believe someone would shoot me for taking their picture so I told him to go to hell, or words to that effect. He chased me, and during that chase, he shot at me, but I managed to dodge him. I took the chip out of the camera and dropped the camera deliberately to let him pick it up. I dodged back and made my way back here."

"Let me have a look at you," Jen said firmly.

"First things first", Cyril said warding her off, as he handed Jeff the chip from the camera, "this is what you needed."

"But not at the expense of getting you shot for Christ's sake", Jeff added.

"It looks worse than it is", Cyril had said, "you just get the bastards that's all I want. Right, you can play and nurse me now Jen", Cyril said.

"Nurse you! I'll knuckle you." Jen said angrily but with great concern, said, "now come on over here, and stop bleeding all over the place. I've just cleaned up", Jen said. And they both looked at the state of their makeshift shelter and smiled.

She very gently washed his wound clucking over him like a mother hen, "Macho men", she said, "thank God it's only a flesh wound, you're going to be sore for a few weeks."

"That bloke in the helicopter obviously didn't want to be seen anywhere near here by the looks of it." Jeff said, "I wonder why? and how come he didn't look in the camera for the chip?"

"He did", Cyril said, "and he would have found one. I swapped an old one for the one I used so he wouldn't know and would just think I dropped the camera as I ran. As soon as he picked the camera up, he stopped chasing me, checked the camera had the chip in it went back to the helicopter and flew off", Cyril chuckled, "good thinking huh?"

"You sail too close to the wind for your own good, you do," Jen replied, "now will you let me see to this wound?" and she continued to fuss over him and dress his wound.

Derek had put his head around the corner, and said, "I heard what happened. This proves that what you've been saying all along is true, otherwise, why would they shoot Cyril?"

Derek continued, "was it that little ginger-haired shit at the Terminal? Because I have a score to settle with him, and I want him first."

"No," said Cyril, "this one had black hair, the one at the Terminal has blonde hair. This one was the one called "Wilson". I saw him earlier when I was there before. Looks like an evil piece of work, and I've met some real nasty people in my time and I'd put him in the top three."

~ *0* ~

"The sooner we get copies of these photographs the better", Jeff said, "so we need to get them done soon."

"Michael knows of a computer shop just on Mainland that his brother owned. He stores computers and fax machines in the basement" Jen said, "I wonder if any are still intact. I'll ask him.

"I know it's important to get these films developed but not if people are going to get hurt, there has been enough death as we saw today", Jeff intervened.

"Where's all this fighting spirit we heard you had?" Jen asked, putting her hands on her hips.

"It's alright if I take the risk, I'm the one that pays the price", Jeff said, "but I can't ask anyone else to pay the price for me when they are taking the risk."

Jen turned on him with her eyes flashing very angrily, "Who the hell do you think you are, telling us we can't take risks, as far as someone paying the price, don't you think those kids you saw in that school today didn't pay the price? It's payback time and I for one will die before those bastards you are after win."

She checked herself, "Sorry, but you men make me so angry when you only want to be the hero on your own, without letting anyone else take some of the strain."

Derek nudged Jeff, and said, "I told you not to upset her and that she had a temper."

"Michael's quite capable of looking after himself", Derek added, "he can use his loaf as well, that's more than can be said for most boxers."

OK then" Jeff submitted, "I stand reprimanded if he can get to his brother's shop, copy the photographs, and then perhaps he can send copies and attach a message via email to contacts I still have in the media. But if he's caught it will go badly for him. He has to know the risks."

"He'll be thinking of those kids who didn't stand a chance, not of his own skin, but I will tell him", Jen said.

Cyril said to Jeff with a sly smile, "Don't you want to see what other presents daddy brought you?"

Handing over a small bundle of papers to Jeff, he added, "I thought they might be important?"

"Where did you get them?" Jeff had asked.

"Well, you know I told you Wilson took all those papers off the dead bodies in the control room, well, he missed the ones under the body of the bloke that sat in the chair at the top of the table, and these are them."

"Brilliant", Jeff said, "I need to study them", so he took the portfolio into a corner, sat down and started reading through the papers.

There was a list of very urgent outstanding maintenance, and repair work that was overdue to be done, all of which had been recommended to be deferred until next year's budget due to the time required getting these items repaired and the downtime, they would incur, creating a loss of revenue. The rest of the papers read like a who's who of the gas industry world.

One separate document spoke of a deal supplying gas at a cheap rate between a right-wing fascist Organisation called "The Senate" and how "UK United Gas" had aligned themselves with the "Senate" also how any company or country that did not align with the "Senate" would be brought to its knees and the companies forced out of business.

It also explained how "The Senate" was going to commandeer all the gas fields under its worldwide organisation and control the flow of gas throughout the world so that they could take over and control different countries one by one.

For giving "The Senate" support Sir William Waits, and UK United Gas would get control of all the energy market within the UK, and Sir William would be the President of the United Kingdom.

These papers were dynamite with a short fuse and he had to keep them safe and get them to John as soon as possible without being caught or the papers found. But how?

Jeff had thought of the little safe in his bungalow, but Wilson's people had been there already so how safe was that? Hang on a minute he mused, if they had already searched his place recently, they were not likely to search it again very soon, so they should be safe there for a while until he could get them to John.

"I need to put this somewhere safe", he said to Jen, these papers are so important, no-one must know where they are, in case they're caught, what they don't know won't hurt them, and I don't trust that Wilson to play by the rules, so I need to go out for a while if you can cover for me."

"If it was anybody else, I'd say go hang", Jen said, "I won't ask what's in the papers but they do seem important to you. If you assure me, they're that important then OK."

Jeff said, "what Cyril got was probably one of the most important documents we need to prove treachery, corruption, and treason, by Sir William Waits and UK United Gas, and the papers need to be kept safe, and the least amount of people that know that we have them, and where they are, the better for now, O.K."

"Do you have a camera that takes the same chip as this one?" Jeff said, "I want to photograph these papers so I can send them on via the net and keep the originals for safekeeping."

"There's one in that cupboard", Derek said, "when Jen asked for a camera, we all had a scratch around and we got three altogether", he got the camera, checked there was a chip in it and gave it to Jeff.

Jeff photographed the papers page by page, then said when he'd finished, "We can send this on with the photos of what's going on here. Later I will have to go out for a while but I won't be long."

"Do you need someone to go with you?" Jen asked.

"Better not, the least known the better", Jeff said and settled down to re-read the papers Cyril had managed to find and waited until much later when it was quiet before he ventured out.

Jen had said, to Jeff, "I gave that chip from the camera to Michael and he's gone to get the prints done and also send them off in your name to your press contacts and that address you spoke of if he can. He said it had to be in your name because they know you, but not him, and you have a reputation for telling the truth to the press."

Jeff had thanked Jen and then said, "I hope he keeps himself safe? He's taking an awful risk for me."

"Hey it's not just for you, it's for those dead kids remember", Jen had retorted, "so rest up before you go."

She left the room and started fussing over Cyril.

In the other room, Cyril said to Jen, "What makes a man like him tick? He takes on the impossible odds for what? What does he get out of it? What's in it for him, financially?"

Jen responded, "He'll get nothing out of this financially, you can bet on that."

"What does he do it for then? Eh!" Cyril replied.

"Principles, moral justice", Jen had answered. "He has a Code he will live or die by."

Then she continued, "I love you for what you are, Cyril. I know you're an old tea leaf and a very good one, but even you would not take an old lady's handbag, you like a much more principled challenge like today that not many other tea leafs could do, right?"

"You would not take an old lady's handbag but you would take gems and paintings from the very rich because you have the ability and principles to achieve it. Well, Jeff has the same sort of principles but in his case, he's much too honest to be a tea leaf and he lives by an old fashion code of principles that you don't see much of now. Integrity, honesty, a gentleman in the right sense of the word and a man of his word, and above all he'll die by his principles and that is a rare trait today."

She continued, "If he believes something is fundamentally wrong he will oppose it and stand up against anyone no matter how much money they have or how powerful they are to protect the less fortunate."

"What! Like some knight in shining armour?" Cyril had scoffed.

"I love you, Cyril, I just admire what he does and why he does it."

Cyril looked at Jen and realised what she had just admitted to, that she loved him still, and he warmed towards her.

Jen continued, "He's just cut from a different cloth that's all, and he's fighting for you, me and what happened to those kids and all those families. We did not ask him. He does it because he believes someone should do something and stand and be counted, not sit back and just let it happen, and then say someone should have done something. Like you're a very good tea leaf, probably the best, he's good at what he does, being a loose cannon",

"He is so good" Jen continued "that UK United Gas has put a price for information on his whereabouts of £1 million."

"A million pounds cash", Cyril whistled, "just for saying where he is?" Cyril said astounded. Then continued, "He must be able to seriously hurt those bastards for them to offer that sort of money.

The help he needs to expose these bastards, he won't ask for", Jen had said angrily, "it has to be offered and given freely with no strings, he has a code of ethics that is rare today, and principles we have lost in this world of today that is full of greed.

He is old fashioned but I wish there were a lot more like him, then this world would be a better place to live in, without the constant attitude of what's in it for me? Jeff will live or die by his Code of ethics.

Jeff accepts people for who they are, and whether they have any principles or not, all he asks is for people to accept. He has his code that he will live or die by."

~ *0* ~

It was about an hour before dusk when Jeff got the gun out of the cycle pannier and hid it in the back of his trousers feeling a lot safer with it, than without it, and left the cellars.

He made his way towards the area where he lived, picking his way over broken buildings and the grotesque horrors that were inside them and lying around outside.

He had just arrived without incident at his bungalow when he heard the throb of the rotors of a helicopter and he dived for cover in a doorway, hoping he had not been seen.

The helicopter circled around once and then passed overhead and headed toward the Terminal.

Jeff had made his way to what was left of his bungalow dreading what he was going to see. He made his way inside the charred remains of the place he had lived and learned to love over many years, bracing himself for the worst.

Everything was scattered about, all his personal possessions that had survived were thrown around as Wilson's henchmen had left them.

Jeff had searched for any sign of his wife but could not find her or her remains and this puzzled him.

He had gone straight to the floor safe that he had. It was open and papers such as his passport and other documents that had been inside had gone.

He took the papers he had with him and put them in the safe and set the combination and locked it.

He had felt that if they had looked here once they were not likely to look again in the same place. If they had already taken his papers that had been inside, they wouldn't be expecting more to be put back in, so, therefore, they should be safe for now until he could get them to John.

He had made his way out of the bungalow and back to the Cellars. As he got near the junction that led him to the cellars, he heard someone call his name softly and it made him jump.

He looked around and spotted Michael making his way towards him. As he got closer, he could see Michael had been in a fight, there was a cut and bruising around his eyes and he had a swollen lip.

"What happened to you?" Jeff asked in a quiet voice.

Michael explained, "After I sent your photos and e-mails, I was coming back when these two goons jumped me. They started asking questions about you and if I had seen you. They had a real bullying attitude and I don't like bullies. So, they tried being Mr nice guy and when that didn't work, they started the rough stuff. I let them think they had softened me up and they then untied me. That was their mistake. They didn't know I never lost a fight in the ring, now they'll be eating out of a straw for months. As I told them and their boss who I also put to sleep when he came in at the end. I don't like bullies."

"I'm sorry I got you into this", Jeff had said,

"Hey, I got myself into this. All I needed was a prod from you, and I'm glad I'm in it. I'm big enough and ugly enough to look after myself as those three found out the hard way, so that's enough from you, right!"

"Thanks anyway", Jeff said.

Michael smiled and said, "Let's get back to the others and bring them up to speed."

As they made their way back Jeff had told Michael about the papers that Cyril had found and what they proved.

Michael whistled, "those bastards want to cover up all these deaths they've caused to further their own ends, it's inhuman", and then he said, "I'm glad I had the chance to get a few blows in for us. If I'd known then what you just told me, they would have been dead by now."

They arrived at the cellars just as the helicopter started taking off from the Terminal so they hurried inside before they were seen.

When Jeff had gotten inside there was a crowd of people there, all eager to see him and asking questions, such as was it true that this was an industrial accident being covered up by "UK United Gas" also, if it was true, how they could help get the bastards.

Jeff said, "I need proof of it going on, and I need to stay alive long enough to expose the truth through the media, which at the moment is the only weapon we have."

Michael said, "We are aware there's a price put on his head by UK United Gas and anybody thinking of trying to get that price answers to me understand?"

"And me and Jen", Derek had said from the back of the room.

Someone also said from the back, "everybody thinks you died at the Community Hall, well that's what the news has been saying."

"My death seems to have been much exaggerated", Jeff has said, laughingly.

Michael butted in, "as far as we're concerned, he is dead, and that's the only way he's going to be able to stay alive, do you understand, because if they find out he's alive before he exposes what's going on, we are all dead."

"Make no mistake, they'll take no prisoners." Jen added, "If they find out there's any evidence to expose them, they'll crush it, and they'll crush the people who they think will do them the most harm. You only have to look at what they did to Cyril because they thought he took a photo of one of them and what they did to Michael when they wanted information. If they can do that and get away with it, they can do anything."

The people murmured and talked amongst themselves and then a woman spoke up and said, "I don't know about the others here but I'm with Jeff. He's always tried to look after the Estuary area and its people and that's good enough for me."

Then the same woman continued, "Where are the few of our so-called elected councillors that survived? Nowhere to be seen that's what. Oh, we've heard them from the comfort of the radio station, trying to say the best plaudits of how terrible it is, but none of them are here to help us. They're all too busy looking after themselves and their own families"

Then another man shouted, "all we ask for is help to get our lives back in some sort of order, and what do we get? We get treated as though we're criminals, the only helicopters that could bring us help have only gone to the Terminal and back and none of them helps us?"

Just then, the throbbing sound of a helicopter started to get closer. They all looked worried and concerned so Jeff had put his head around the door frame to see if he could see what was going on. Just at that moment, the helicopter made a pass overhead, he ducked back in, and was listening intently.

Above the throbbing noise of the rotor blades of the helicopter, Jeff heard the sound of small arms gunfire, and a young man and a young woman near a burned-out car which was across the road fell to the road, shot.

The passenger in the helicopter was laughing as he took potshots at the rest of the people in the group that were trying to hide from the bullets, he was spraying at them from his automatic pistol and laughing.

"You, sick bastard", Jeff had yelled, and ran outside, drew his gun which he had tucked into the back of his belt, aimed and fired two shots at the man in the helicopter.

Two things happened very quickly.

More by luck than judgment the two shots Jeff fired, one had hit the passenger with the automatic pistol, the passenger fell out of the helicopter bleeding from a chest wound and screaming all the way to the ground where he bounced off the burnt-out car and crashed in a heap and did not move.

The second shot had hit the engine of the helicopter, the helicopter's engine had started smoking and the rotors juddered and the engine started coughing. It had started pitching and yawing then the pilot managed to get control and flew the helicopter away. It managed a distance of about a mile before it plunged to the ground and burst into flames.

A cheer went up from the people around the cellars.

"Good shooting", Derek said, "where did you learn to shoot like that? I'm impressed."

"We had a gun range in the bank where I worked, they had a gun club which I belonged to", Jeff replied.

"But they were good shots", Derek insisted.

"More luck than judgment", Jeff had said, "now let's see if those people he was shooting at survived."

When they got to the burned-out car they saw a young lad and a young girl, no more than 14-15 years old dead in a pool of blood. They hadn't stood a chance, they had been shot down for sport.

"Bastards", Derek said, with hate in his voice, "see what identity the bloke has on him"

Derek kicked the body of the passenger of the helicopter and the man moaned. Jeff ran over to examine his injuries, "who sent you?" Jeff asked angrily.

The man refused to say anything.

Jeff grabbed the man and pressed his thumb into the bullet wound, the man screamed, "who sent you?" Jeff insisted.

"Wilson" the man replied weakly and then died.

"What identity has he got on him?" Jeff asked.

Derek searched the man, a set of keys to a car, a security door pass card, a driving licence, a wad of money, a gun and two spare clips and a letter of authorisation to shoot looters on sight signed by none other than Sir William Waits Derek said, "We get hunted down and shot at for wanting to survive. But to them we're sport and a bullet is a lot cheaper than the cost of supporting survivors."

'What gives Sir William the right to authorise men to shoot looters on sight unless he has taken over the country already', Jeff thought, or he's confident that he will very soon. If that is the case, John and the PM were in trouble and so was he, and he had to work fast and get back. He had to use the mobile phone to contact John or Sergeant Dick to see how the situation overall is.

"Let's have that stuff it might be useful", Jeff said to Derek.

When they got back to the cellars, Jeff went into a quiet corner and used the mobile phone and called the number that Sergeant Dick had given him, whilst Derek told everyone what had happened down by the burnt-out car.

A voice at the other end of the phone asked, "Who is this?" Without giving his name Jeff asked for John. The voice on the other end said again, "Who is this and how did you get this number?" Jeff asked for John again and added that if he wasn't there, he would speak to Sergeant Dick instead.

It went quiet at the other end of the phone then a voice which he recognised as John's said, "Yes, who is this? And how did you get this number?"

"It's Jeff", Jeff said, "I need to let you know what's happening."

John said, "Dad, how many times have I told you not to call me at work, you know I'm busy."

Jeff said, "It's not your dad it's me, Jeff."

John said, "yes dad, I did tell you to let me know if there was any change in mum's condition but I only gave you this number for emergencies only.

Jeff said, "you can't talk very much can you because someone's there?"

"That's right dad", John answered, "now you're on the phone how can I help you?"

Jeff, briefly explained to John what he had found out so far and about the shootings.

"O.K," John said, "thanks dad for letting me know how mum is. I'll certainly try to see you and mum at the weekend but I have to go now. I have to fly to investigate a helicopter crash in a couple of hours. I know you were into aeroplane crash investigations before you retired, you would find it interesting if you could have been there. And we could have had a drink in the Cellars, and by the way, I will pick you up your favourite tobacco at the same time on my way back, so don't worry, bye for now and I will see you and mum soon, alright?"

Before John had rung off, Jeff could hear him talk to someone at the other end of the phone, "Sorry about that P.M., but my dad worries about mum a lot, and he thinks I should be informed every time she has a bad turn, then the phone clicked off.

Jeff thought, boy that was cryptic, so, he's coming here, and he's already heard about the helicopter crash that has just happened, that was fast. He needs to see me but how? How can that happen without breaking cover, and if he is coming to the Cellars, Jeff, he needs to get everyone clear of it.

He turned to Cyril but before he could say anything further Cyril said, "I see you got one of the bastards, and that shot at the helicopter putting it out of action was brilliant. They'll think twice before messing with us again."

"They already know what happened", Jeff had said.

"What!" said Cyril, "they can't have, it's only just happened."

"I think the pilot got a "MAYDAY" out before he hit the ground hard, not only that, but they're going to come and investigate the helicopter crash within the next couple of hours, plus we need to make sure this place looks unoccupied also I need to meet this person that is coming, and he is going to help us get these bastards for good."

"You move in strange circles Jeff", said Cyril warily, "if it was anyone else, I wouldn't trust them, but after what you did for those young kids who were just trying to survive, you got my support in whatever you decide."

Cyril continued, "That bastard shot those kids for sport and deserved to die, unfortunately, he died too quickly for my liking. All I hope is that the pilot dies too and if he does, I hope he dies slowly and in agony. Bloody Sick bastards."

Cyril said, with venom, "what they did out there shows what they think of us and how we can't trust them. I thought we got rid of the Hitler and fascists of this world, but it looks like we still need to exterminate a few more that have just crawled out of the woodwork."

Jen said, "I heard what you said to Cyril about us having visitors and I agree with you, we need to get these people out of here or they could get hurt, I'll have a word with them, because if they talk it would blow your cover and probably get them killed as well.

How's your arm?" Jen then asked Cyril.

"Stop fussing woman", Cyril said, "I'll live, that's more than those poor bastards out there will, sick bastards. They never stood a chance."

"Right, let's get things moving", Jen said and went to organise the people, where they were to go for now, and also to make the area look as though it had not been lived in.

People drifted off in ones and twos, gradually there was only Jeff, Derek, Jen, and Cyril remaining in the building.

Derek said, "I'll be in that house over there watching in case you need help."

Jen said to Cyril, "you need some TLC and I know the place for that, so come on wounded hero."

"Now don't you embarrass me, woman", Cyril responded, "I might have to spank you."

"When you're a big enough boy you might try", Jen answered Cyril smartly, with a twinkle in her eye, "come on, we don't want to be seen by Jeff's visitor, and Derek will make sure Jeff is safe, come on you need nursing", and grabbed his hand and they left and Derek went with them.

Jeff was left alone with his thoughts of how it had all come to this situation of violence and the deaths of thousands of innocent people, all caught up in the machinations of a megalomaniac like "Sir William Waits" who wanted to be a dictator and did not care how he achieved his aim or who died so he could totally dominate the country. Talk about power corrupts, absolute power corrupts absolutely.

~ 0 ~

Jeff heard the throbbing of the rotors of a helicopter getting closer and he tucked himself into an alcove, from where he had a good view of the doorway without being seen. He drew the gun from where it was tucked in the back of his trousers and settled down to wait and to see who would be turning up.

After he had heard the sound of the helicopter drawing nearer, he had an uneasy thought! What had happened to the body of the man who he had shot and who had fallen out of the helicopter? They surely must see it, unless Derek had moved it.

The sound of the helicopter overhead got much louder and dust started to blow around from the downward wash of the rotor blades. The engine of the helicopter slowed and the rotors whirled slowly on tick over.

Jeff could hear a muffled voice that seemed to be giving instructions. After a little while there was a scrambling noise over some of the rubble by the door. Jeff peered through the dust to see John standing by the doorway.

'Can I get any tobacco here?' John whispered,

Jeff slid out from the alcove holding the gun, "Are you alone?" Jeff asked equally quietly.

"Apart from the pilot of the helicopter", John said, "and he's under instructions not to leave the helicopter for any reason if something happens to me, he is to take off straight away, and detonate a device over this area then return back and report what has happened."

"You're expendable as well then?" Jeff exclaimed, "That's a bluff."

"No, it isn't. either you have something important for me, or I leave now", John said, "the situation is poised on a knife-edge, and it could go either way."

"O.K." said Jeff, "that helicopter crash, did the pilot survive?"

"No, he didn't! What do you know about that? John asked suspiciously, this is a restricted area, there have been no authorised flights near this area since the incident."

"Well those bastards were taking potshots at a couple of kids for fun and laughed when they shot them dead, I got a couple of lucky shots in, one put the passenger out of his misery and I hit something in the engine, the pilot crashed over there, and I hoped he had died too", Jeff continued, "and as far as there being no authorised flights in this area, they have landed in the Terminal or on the roof of the Terminal at least a dozen times, and they have a henchman in the Terminal site threatening to shoot anyone who goes near it."

"They are not my people", John added, "plus I thought you were not going to draw attention to yourself, be discreet and find out information, not advertise to all and sundry you were here? I've had a hell of a job to keep that crash quiet for now …. I've not got long, as far as the pilot knows I am reminiscing about having a good time with my dad here years ago, so what have you found out so far?"

Jeff told him about the visits to the Terminal by Wilson and a few others.

"Wilson came here? He wouldn't dare unless they were very desperate!" John said, "but I'll have to take your word for it as you obviously can't prove it?"

"But I can!" Jeff replied heatedly, "there is a clear photograph taken of him by the Terminal in his helicopter, and Wilson shot at the person who took the photograph. It's on the email attachment we sent to your email address which you gave me, along with a photograph of the papers seized by us that were at the Terminal in the Board Room."

"Wilson would shoot anyone who saw him", said John, "he can't be seen anywhere near here, as that links him directly with UK United Gas and Sir William Waits. If he thinks you have a photograph of him here, he will kill you for it."

Jeff explained the circumstances of how the picture was taken and how Wilson believed he had the camera and the chip, also about the papers and what was in them that was found under the body in the Board Room. Jeff did let John know he had them in a safe place and he had hidden them for safekeeping. He told him how Wilson had destroyed all the meeting papers and broken the dials and clocks in the control room of the Terminal and how he thought the incident happened by the scorch marks on the seawall.

John said, "I need those documents to link it all together, where are they?"

"They're safe", Jeff said, "but you have the photographs of them to prove they exist"

"Don't you trust me?" John asked, forcing a note of quite a childish hurt into his voice.

"Those papers are the people's safe ticket, and I'm not going to give that away", Jeff answered firmly.

"Don't play hardball with me, matey, I invented the game", John warned.

"I need guarantees for the people here. And all the time I hold those papers no more people are going to be shot as a sport", Jeff said, "and they also get the help they need."

"The emergency forces are stretched to breaking point and working their way towards you as we speak but there is a lot of devastation and victims to clear away first. Now I can't give any guarantees", John said.

"You can make things happen, I know you can", Jeff said, "you or the P.M. can make sure Sir William Waits guarantees their safety and pulls in the neck of Wilson and his cronies.

Sir William and his cronies are trying to take control of this country and if they succeed, you'll have a jackboot on your neck", John said coolly, "and there's nothing I can do to stop that."

"Whose side are you on anyway?" Jeff asked sarcastically, "Sir William's people are trying to clear away any evidence of their involvement as fast as possible, and your people do nothing but work slowly from the outside inwards clearing the ground as you go."

Jeff added, "by the time you do get around to doing something here, Wilson and Sir William will have wiped away any sign of it being an accident caused by his greed for which he alone is responsible, did you also know he is being backed by a group calling themselves "The Senate" and he will have made political gains and blamed terrorists and got control of this country."

Jeff insisted, "when that happens, and this group calling themselves the "Senate" takes over, does the last one leaving the country switch the lights off because this will not be Great Britain anymore, but a fascist state."

"Who is this group you call "The Senate" and what do you see being done about them?" John asked.

"Firstly, get some support to these people and stop Sir William's men from tampering with the evidence at the Terminal", Jeff replied.

"I need evidence of this tampering before I can confront them", John said.

"I sent you copies of the papers and Wilson's photograph to that email address you gave me. those papers should condemn him on their own", Jeff said.

"Ok, I accept that," said John, "now where are those papers?"

"Safe", Jeff reiterated again dismissively.

"Did I tell you we found your wife and daughter alive at a health farm?" John suddenly volunteered this startling piece of information, just as though it was some kind of carrot being dangled in front of a donkey.

"Are they alright and safe?" Jeff asked quickly, automatically pulling a mask of careful blankness over his features.

"They are as safe as those papers are", John said. His meaning was very clear.

"How come my wife and daughter were not in the Estuary when it went up?" Jeff asked, suddenly,

"Apparently, they were at a health spa as your daughter had got a last-minute cancellation that morning and took your wife with her", John answered, "but, as I said, they are safe for now. But no-one must know they are alive otherwise they can use them to get to you."

"They are safe, that I guarantee, as you guarantee those papers are safe, do we understand one another?"

It was then that Jeff remembered that his wife had said something about their daughter trying to get a cancellation but he had been on the phone at the time and then had been engrossed in the paperwork he was doing and had not listened to all what she had said.

He felt overwhelming relief and happiness for himself and terrible sadness for the families of the loved ones that had not escaped the terrible chain of events that had led to so many deaths.

"As long as my family is safe, those papers are safe", said Jeff, "and I am aware how bad you need those papers, so, if anything happens to my family those papers will be destroyed, that I can also guarantee. so, we understand one another."

"You still don't trust anybody, do you?" John commented, "Ok, well you really can trust me."

"We'll see", said Jeff.

Jeff then went on to tell him about the conversation between Wilson and the other man at the Terminal in reference to the green Jaguar car at the Councillor's house.

"My brother is going to be very interested in that information. Look. Things are not quite in place at the moment to act on and stop our friends, but they will be soon", John said, "I must go now if I'm not to make the pilot suspicious."

"I'll send some parcels for you all, that's the best I can do for now, but I will give your regards to your wife and daughter in the meanwhile. The mobile you have, destroy it, and use this one", John said, handing him a similar Mobil phone "but only use it once, and only once, it is a burn phone, using the number pre-set into it and then destroy it so you can't be traced. I'll send you another one with the parcels. Do exactly the same with that one. Sorry about the cloak and dagger attitude but at the moment it's for the best." Then John added, "you can trust me, Jeff, you really can, now I must go", and he left.

Jeff heard the helicopter's engine fade into the distance and he was left alone with his mind in a spin. He was elated his wife was alive!

As the reality hit him, he was suddenly overwhelmed with depression, sadness and grief for those who had lost everything but mixed with hope for the others and himself and the desperate situation that he was in and also putting others in.

He shook himself out of his depression and mentally told himself off for feeling sorry for himself as there were other people considerably worse off than himself. Clearing his mind of personal matters, he sat back and analysed his situation and what he had to do from here.

~ *0* ~

It was dark by the time Jen and Cyril arrived back at the building and they both had a twinkle in their eyes. Jeff smiled at them thinking that at least out of all this chaos somebody had found happiness even if only for a short while.

"Well, what did your friend have to say?" Jen asked.

Jeff felt that he could not tell them about his wife being alive yet, not with all the loss and sadness they were holding inside, plus all the death and destruction around them, he felt it was the wrong time.

He told them of the parcel drop that was due and what he had told John.

"At least we will get some decent food and the threat of us being eliminated for fun will stop", Cyril said.

"Oh, we'll probably get the food but don't relax against the threat from Wilson and his cronies", Jeff said, "I don't trust that one as far as the end of my nose."

"What do we do now?" Jen asked.

"Take photographs of everything you can and try to record details so it can be used as evidence later, information gathering is what we need to do", Jeff replied.

"Won't the forensic people do that?" Jen queried.

"They will only be able to study what they see when they get here", Jeff said, "and if Wilson and his mob alter the evidence, then that's the evidence they will investigate and then reach the conclusion that Wilson wants them to come to, so it will be one giant cover-up and that's what they're doing at the terminal now, altering the evidence to suit themselves and trying to get themselves off the hook."

"That's criminal", Jen snapped, horrified.

"Not if you don't get caught doing it", Jeff said, "so we have to catch them and record it in any way we can, so as to make them pay for all these deaths, but make no mistake, it will not be easy and it could be very dangerous. If they find out what we are doing it will be curtains, so if anybody wants to say no, I will understand. All I ask is that you just accept that I'm going to do what it takes to put these bastards away forever."

"And you think you can do it on your own?" Jen retorted, raising an eyebrow.

"If that's what it takes, then yes", Jeff answered.

"Typical male", Jen said, "I told you before if you think you can do this on your own you've got another thing coming. Who gave birth to those kids who are dead in the schools? Who watched over them through their illnesses? Who has had to watch them die horribly? Us women, that's who."

Jen retorted, "do you have any idea what it's like to see your child die and not be able to do anything about it? So don't tell me or any other mother she can't help put these bastards in hell, and whether you like it or not, women are a match for any man", Jen said angrily, "you male chauvinistic pig"

"Whoa! I didn't say you couldn't help lady, all I said was it would be dangerous for you", Jeff said placatingly, holding up his hands in submission.

"And women can't face danger?" Jen queried angrily.

"Back off you two", Cyril said, "you know you'll both do what it takes to nail these bastards as will the rest of us, so don't ruffle each other's feathers, the enemy is out there, not inside here, right?"

"Yes" Jen and Jeff said together very sheepishly and smiled at one another looking rather foolish. They both voiced apologies at the same time, and then laughed again.

"Now, what's to be done? and what's the best way of doing it?" Cyril asked.

"Well, we need to get as many trusted people together as possible" Jeff said, "and find out who will, or can do what. We must know our limitations or we'll overstretch ourselves and get caught. If that happens there will be no mercy because these animals play for keeps. We might also have to find another safe place to meet if they find out that we operate from here."

"Leave that to me", Cyril said, "I'll hunt around.

We need to make a list of the type of things that will be of importance, such as photographs of any alterations carried out by them, or any papers that might be of importance, and photographs or descriptions of any of the people attending the site before the investigation team arrive, and if someone has the stomach for it, possible photographs of the inside of the schools and the surrounding areas but above all, nobody must be caught doing it."

Cyril said, "I have been thinking and I might have a list of safe places soon, but to let you know they are safe when you approach them, how's this for an idea? You will see the moving feature that is the sign of a windmill. They are so well known in the Estuary, nobody takes any notice of them (there are lots of them all over the place, in gardens, on churches, on the apex of houses). If the vanes of the windmill are in the shape of a kiss it's safe, if, in the shape of a cross, it's not safe."

"What a brilliant idea", Jeff said.

"It's so obvious, it's foolproof, and it's right under their noses", Cyril continued, "I read it in a book once. It was a system adopted by an underground movement during the Second World War in Holland."

"Ok. In the morning we get going, but don't get caught", Jeff said and they settled down for the night.

Jeff sat in the corner, his mind in a spin. His wife was safe, thank God. He wanted to be with her but there was a price on his head and until this was over, they were expendable so instead, he concentrated on trying to put everything in order of priority. The more information he got the better, but at the same time, he had to keep that information safe, and then send it to John, and hope John's side won. If not, he was dead and buried but he already knew he had made the choice of whose side he was on.

He drifted off to sleep mulling these things over.

~ 0 ~

He was shaken awake by Derek whilst it was still dark.

"What's the matter?" Jeff asked as he became instantly alert.

"There are troops moving around up the road and they're not the usual pickets stationed near here, we need to be out of here in case they come here."

"What time is it?" Jeff asked.

"Just gone 6 am", Derek said, "come on move, if you don't want to be caught."

They made their way past the graveyard towards what was the central area of the Estuary, keeping an eye on what the squad of troops that were dressed in black uniforms were doing all the time.

The troops seemed to be looking for survivors gathering them together and taking them away in trucks to what was the Sports Centre area at the main junction to the mainland.

They made their way slowly along the ditches and dykes, using the blackened stumps of the hedgerows as cover and made their way towards the Sports Centre area making sure they were not seen.

When they got to the derelict building that housed the swimming pool, they crept to the corner of the building and from there they could see and hear what was going on.

Jeff heard his name mentioned and something about a reward then a couple of the troopers started slapping some of the women around.

Just then a young man ran from the group towards where they lay hidden. Bullets promptly spat up from where he had been running and the lad stopped in his tracks and put his hands up.

Then what seemed to be some sort of officer shouted to two troopers, teach him a lesson not to mess with us.

Two troopers broke away from the group and went over to the lad and started pushing and punching him to the ground.

The lad broke free and ran directly to where Jeff and Derek lay hidden.

He ran around the corner of the building into Jeff's arms with the two troopers following.

Jeff grabbed the young lad, pulled him to one side, put his hand over his mouth to stop him from yelling.

Jeff heard two grunts as the two troopers hit the deck out cold with Derek standing over them ready to hit them again.

"Quickly, get their guns and grenades", Derek ordered in a whisper, at the same time motioning the lad to stay quiet.

Jeff put his head to the corner to see if anyone had heard them. What he saw shocked him.

The people were lined up and the officer was questioning them violently and pushing his gun into their stomachs repeatedly with a very threatening manner. He was indicating that if they did not tell him what he wanted to know he would shoot them or their loved ones who stood next to them.

Then Jeff saw a lorry loaded with ammunition boxes pull up facing them. The driver ran round to the back of the lorry and joined the other man in the back of the lorry where they uncovered a machine gun and pointed it at the people that were lined up ready for a firing squad.

"We have to do something fast, they are going to execute and kill them all", Jeff whispered urgently to Derek, "follow my lead", and he grabbed a rifle and some grenades and ran towards the truck. He made it to the truck without being seen with Derek close behind him. He signalled to Derek that they needed to get the two troopers off of the truck and disarmed.

Derek climbed onto the truck from the driver's side, slid up behind the two troopers that were talking loudly and were busy drooling and being very graphic on what they wanted to do to two of the young girls standing there terrified. The troopers did not hear him until he hit them with the butt of his gun. They instantly slumped to the floor of the truck then they rolled onto the ground unconscious.

The noise of the two troopers hitting the ground startled the officer. He instantly came towards them with his gun raised and snarled, "Who the hell are you? Wait a minute, you're the man I'm looking for", gesturing towards Jeff.

"Well you found me and if you don't lay down your arms, I'll drop these armed grenades into this ammunition truck and we'll all die", Jeff said.

"I can shoot and kill you from here very easily", the officer said lightly.

"Then I drop the grenades anyway and take you and your squad with me, that seems a fair exchange", Jeff returned, equally lightly. "Everyone thinks I am dead anyway, this time I have the opportunity to take you with me."

The officer's face was a picture of uncertainty. Finally, he said to his men over his shoulder, "put down your gun's men, now", he ordered.

Then Jeff said to the men in the group of people, "disarm them and you don't have to be gentle."

When the troopers were disarmed and rounded up along with the officer, the frightened officer said, you can't kill us, I was only following orders from

Sir William Waits, the new president-elect, he gave orders to get you at any cost and these people might have known where you were."

"So, you were going to kill them if they didn't tell you what they didn't know?" Jeff said.

"I was only following orders as were my men", the officer blurted out.

"In the Second World War the guards said the same about the death camps", Jeff said.

"Right, order your men to drop their trousers round their ankles but not to take them off.

The officer looked at him strangely, but surprisingly volunteered no argument and gave the order.

"Your men can't run anywhere or go after these people with their pants down and their hands tied behind their backs and all bundled together", Jeff explained.

When the two troopers that had been on the truck had had now come too, they were also ordered to do the same and had their hands tied up. The two troopers that Derek put to sleep with a hay-maker were dragged back to the fold and tied up with the rest.

The two young girls that the two troopers had boasted about, came over to the two tied up troopers that were now coming to and kicked them in the crotch very hard and they doubled over in agony.

"Animals!" they said and spat on them viciously.

"Did you see what those two girls did to my men?" the officer complained to Jeff.

"No, I didn't see anything", Jeff said, "the same as you obviously didn't see anything when you were controlling your troopers."

Realising he was not going to die there and then, the officer started feeling brave again, and said to Jeff, "You'll get yours when Wilson finds you alive, and out what you've done."

Before Jeff could answer, Derek stepped in and hit the officer with a roundhouse punch that laid him flat on his back with a crunch then said to Jeff, "If his brain was taxed he would get a rebate", then looking down on the man said, "well, you've got yours now for being a bully, and that's what Wilson will get if I catch up with him."

Jeff turned to the people and said, "you need to get out of here and you better use the trucks and head to a safer area and try to avoid the troopers in black", he shouted. "We do have troops in the area but they are not in black, they will aid you."

"What about them?" a man asked from the rear of the group.

"Tie them up tightly and leave them to the worms, were they going to show you any mercy? No. I suggest we do the same for them, so leave them as they are and let their people find them but take a note of all their names and keep that information safe so that it can be used at a later date if there is a crimes tribunal. Now we have to go", Jeff said. "Keep safe and look out for any more troopers."

"Thank you two for doing what you did", a man said; "we won't forget it. I'm sure they would have killed us men and done God knows what to the women, and those two made their intentions known," the same man said pointing to the two men still rolling in agony from the kick in the crotch. "They still had that uncontrolled animal look about them." Then the man added, "don't worry, we'll deal with these scums in our own way", pointing to the sorry sight of troopers huddled together trying not to look sheepish, silly and undignified with their trousers round their ankles and their hands tied behind their backs.

"If the rule of law has broken down, avoid the black troopers, and look for our soldiers, you should be safer with them", Jeff said, "good luck."

"Come on you, ugly brute", Jeff said, jokingly to Derek, "they don't need us anymore."

"Ok," Derek said slapping him on the back and sending him flying, "We make a good team you and me, a dynamic duo, eh!"

"More like beauty and the beast, and you're no beauty", Jeff rejoined smirking.

Derek laughed heartily, slapped him on the back again and said, "I like you, let's go, and by the way where are we going?"

"Councillor Randle's house", Jeff answered.

"What! That means we have to pass the picket line", said Derek.

"Not if we go via the seaward side of the barrier at the Creek", Jeff replied, "and with them looking after the trucks of people that are going pass there now, they won't see us."

~ 0 ~

They made their way across the creek flood barrier onto the mainland and onto Councillor Randle's house without incident.

As they passed on the seaward side of the Barrier, they could see in the distance soldiers stopping the trucks then escorting their passengers away. Jeff had a feeling that the people would now be safe.

They made their way and approached Councillor Randle's house via the back garden then made their way to the concealed garage to find it empty with the doors open, the green Jaguar that Cyril had spoken of was gone, so they made their way carefully into the house.

The place looked as though it had been turned over by professional people looking for something important. The place had been ransacked.

They went into another room to see a safe that was fixed to the wall open, it was empty, most of the contents had been riffled through completely and paperwork was scattered on the floor.

The body of Councillor Randle lay twisted in a grotesque heap his neck obviously snapped as his head lay at a peculiar angle.

"Looks like there's no honour amongst thieves", Jeff retorted. Looking at Councillor Randle's body.

Derek went over to the safe, "Bloody empty", he stated in a disgusted tone.

Jeff looked at him and said, "Strange that he has the same type of safe I have, but his is a much more sophisticated model. I couldn't afford this type, it's too expensive, no difference in looks from the outside, but I believe this one had an extra compartment at the back."

Jeff put his hand inside the safe and felt around. He then pushed the back of the safe and something clicked inside. The back wall of the safe slid across revealing another compartment in which was papers, passports under different names but with Councillor Randle's picture on them and numerous different currencies and a bag of gold sovereigns.

"I bet whoever rifled this safe didn't know about this compartment. The only reason I know about it is because at the time when I had one put in I could not afford this model, it was a hell of a lot dearer but the salesman showed it to me to try to get me to buy it."

"Here you can have the sovereigns if you want", Jeff said, tossing the bag of coins to Derek, "he's past caring", pointing to the body of Councillor Randle, "I need to see what's in this paperwork", Jeff took out the papers and started to study them closely.

After a while, Jeff paused and whistled "Jesus Christ!" what he'd found opened a can of worms for sure. The papers named names and linked all the conniving lot together, there were records of payments to officials and how much, and when they got paid, the papers were linking officials that went all the way to the top people in planning and Government and Whitehall circles.

No wonder they wanted Randle dead. He held them all to ransom all the way to Sir William Waits and Whitehall and more. The papers tied and linked in nicely with the papers that he had given to John when he first met him in the police station.

"This is dynamite with a capital D", Jeff said, "we need to copy these and send them to John."

"Who's John?" Derek asked.

"The Government man who visited me in the helicopter" Jeff responded.

"Are you playing me for a sucker?" Derek said to Jeff very menacingly.

"No", Jeff said and sat down and went through all that had happened to him up until the time they had met.

"Now you see why they want me dead, and anyone who knows as much as I do along with me."

"So, I'm on their hit list as well", Derek said, "nice to be popular." He broke into a great big beaming smile.

"We have to send this on, and then keep the papers safe for our own protection", Jeff said,

"I do believe you don't trust anybody in high office, not even this John bloke! Do you?" Derek mused.

"My old man always said to me 'walk gently in this world son but carry a big stick just in case", Jeff said, "I trust these people about as far as the end of my nose, and at this moment in time no further, but of all the options I have, John is the better one, and is at least, trying to stop Sir William and his sidekick Watson taking over the country and covering up mass murder."

"Let's make our way to Michael's brother's computer place and see if we can copy these documents", Derek said "then we can send them off to this John. I know the way it's not very far."

It took a while but they made their way without incident by using the back roads and hedgerows for cover they dove for cover at the slightest noise on two occasions but they made it safely.

Just as they neared Michael's brother's computer place, they heard a scraping noise and that immediately alerted both men as they ducked down.

They crept forward and slowly entered the basement of the building.

"God, You two scared the life out of me", Michael said, "as he appeared from behind a cabinet."

Both Jeff and Derek were also startled, and Derek said, "what are you doing here?"

"I was checking to see if the fax machine and the copier were still working knowing you were going to need them."

"Well, are they?" Jeff asked.

"Yes", Michael said.

"Good, we need to send some stuff right now, it was lucky you were here", Jeff replied. "You can help us."

He got out the papers he had got from Councillor Randle's safe passing them to Michael to fax off to the number he gave him and then started copying the pages.

Michael, looked at some of the pages as he was copying them and said, "Christ on a crutch! You got this from Councillor Randle's safe? Tell me this is a joke! This information will have repercussions right across the political arena, it names who's involved right up the political ladder and right into Whitehall. If this gets out these people on this list will be destroyed. You say Randle was murdered because of these documents?"

"It looks that way", Jeff Said.

Michael added, "Well if they find out you have them, they will want your head on a pole, no wonder there's a price on your head, and ours also by now. Now we know what this is all about."

As they were finishing and getting to the last page, they heard a noise outside the front of the building.

Men were shouting and there was the stamping of boots.

Michael looked through the basement skylight and said, "We had better move, and now. There's a squad of troopers outside dressed in black, and they look as though they're coming in here, go by the back door and leave everything and run."

Jeff grabbed the papers and joined Derek at the basements back door they were quickly followed closely by Michael just as the front door came crashing in, followed by troopers who were confused as to what they were doing there and what they were looking for and started smashing everything in the building.

The three of them ran out of the basement of the building and along the hedgerow, the way they ran from the building, they could not be seen from the building, and slowly made there way back to the lower part of the Creek to the Barrier, they hoped to cross the creek and onto the relative safety of the Estuary.

"Did you get those papers sent off?" Jeff asked Michael when they were sitting in the alcove of a burnt-out building, they were recovering from their mad dash away from the basement of the building.

"At least it seems that we were not seen,' Derek said, "otherwise there would have been a hue and cry."

"All except the last page, as they came in the door upstairs, I grabbed the documents and disconnected the call", Michael answered.

"Hopefully they won't think of tracing who we made the connection to", Derek said hopefully.

"They can't, it's on a loop, it would take a computer buff to track that connection", Michael said.

"What do you mean?" Jeff asked,

"Well, when the fax lines were connected, it was done on a secure scrambled line. I don't know how my cousin did it, so providing the connection was terminated before they got to the fax machine it can't be tracked or traced."

"The only thing is", Jeff said, "I might have missed faxing the last few copies but we have the original documents with us."

They then made their way slowly back towards the seaward side of Creek, there seemed to be more activity about but not enough to stop them slipping through picket lines.

There also seemed to be a lot of movement on the bridge upstream of the flood barrier in the Creek. They made their way over the Creek via the downstream side of the barrier just as it was getting dark. It had been a long day.

"I need to put these papers away somewhere safe", Jeff said, "wait for me near the Cellars", and he left and made his way to the safe in the floor of his devastated bungalow.

As he approached the building, he kept a wary eye out, but there was nothing untoward and it all looked as though it was the same as he had left it.

He opened his floor safe, put the papers in the safe, closed it then sprinkled some dust and small bits of rubble over the safe to make it look as though it had not been disturbed. Then he made his way to the Cellars.

As he approached the Cellars Derek appeared from nowhere and suddenly pushed Jeff to the ground.

"What the hell was that for?" Jeff asked, in a decidedly put out voice.

"Look at the windmills in the garden", Derek whispered hastily.

Sure enough, they were in the shape of a cross.

"Christ, I nearly walked into that", Jeff hissed.

"So, did I", Derek replied, "but the neighbours are noisy and restless", pointing to a faint movement near the wall approaching the Cellars.

Michael has gone to the Central Garden area to suss out the situation there.

Just then, there was an explosion as a grenade exploded near the Cellars and a few troopers rushed forward out of hiding.

"It's a bloody fox you got, you stupid bastard", one of the Troopers crowed, "so much for getting them with your booby trap."

Then added, "Wilson will do his nut getting him out on a wild goose chase just because you insist on using your poaching skills to catch our friends."

As they both lay hidden, it was a little while later they heard the engine of a jeep approaching. It pulled up and out jumped Wilson and said, "Well what happened here?"

In the glow of the fire, the men have huddled around, Jeff could make out his enemy. It was the first time Jeff had seen the man who was hunting him.

Wilson was about 5ft 10ins, very stocky with cropped hair and had an evil look in his eyes, he looked very powerful and a very nasty piece of work.

"Jones set up a booby trap to catch the rebels", the Sergeant in charge of the troops said very apologetically, "all he got was a fox."

Wilson, menacingly went to Jones and said, "have you got an infinite space between the ears? I need them unharmed for questioning. They now have important papers from Councillor Randle's place and I need to find those papers.

Whilst I don't care what you do to them or their women but I need to be able to question them, not pick up their pieces from the surrounding trees because you want to play poacher, you're not mentally qualified for handicap parking', now get out of my sight."

A second Jeep pulled up and the officer they had seen at the sports center got out.

"Not a very good day for you is it? It looks like the lights are on, but no one's at home", Wilson retorted to him, "firstly you let a small number of civilians overwhelm you, leave you tied up with your trousers round your ankles, they take your guns, and escape to the police authorities. Then we find that Councillor Randle's house your squad was supposed to be guarding was broken into and papers we needed to keep secret were taken."

"Then quite by chance on a raid I carried out in a computer shop I find some copies of the original pages of these documents we are looking for left on a copier. Now I leave you and your men on stakeout duty to see if we can catch any of them if they come back and you advertise that you're here, by letting off a grenade, great.

Anymore stupidity in your family, or is it God has a sense of humour and you're the proof?" Wilson ranted, "Is all the stupidity here in one box?"

"Now you've destroyed the element of surprise you better get your men to stand down and tell them to make safe any booby traps in case they blow themselves up and advertise this covert operation to police and army authorities."

"Aren't we under martial law orders from the Government? And don't the police authorities take orders from us? So why is this operation so covert?" the officer asked.

"You ask too many questions. You take your orders from me, and if you don't like it, I can remove you from command now", Wilson said drawing a gun and pointing at the officer, "and you and your family will go to the camps, is that understood?

Now get your men squared away, or do I relieve you of your command", Wilson said threateningly.

"Sir!" the officer responded hastily then added, "I will get the men squared away now sir."

Then he barked, "Jones! Front and Centre. Get these men squared away and if you as so much as breath wrong, I'll nail you to the wall, understand?"

Derek whispered, "That was close. We need to find a safe place to bed down."

"Wait a minute, let's see what Wilson does?" Jeff whispered, placing a restraining hand on Derek's shoulder.

"I'm off, I have other irons in the fire, and thank Christ I don't have to rely on you", Wilson said, "and don't disturb me unless you have any of them in custody", He got into the jeep and drove off.

"Nasty bastard Colin", a sergeant retorted to the officer, then added, "when I signed up for this lot, it was to protect the country from terrorists, not to beat up and bully my own people. I can't say I'm happy about that, also, how come we've never received written orders confirming Wilson's authority."

The man continued, "We only have his word for it and have you thought from what we hear that Jeff bloke might be right, and if that's the case we're in deep shit, and those people that humiliated us, they would have killed us all if it wasn't for him. And, we would have deserved it for the way the men acted until you and I stopped them. Those girls were right they acted like animals."

"That's enough Sergeant Bates, we agreed to the money we are paid to do this job, so don't question orders, we have to obey them until we know otherwise, understood?"

"Yes, but not to the point of being robots for some megalomaniac", Sergeant Bates said, "that's how "Hitler" started."

"That's enough, I said, you don't want me to tell Wilson, you now want out because you think the going is getting tough, and you are now having second thoughts?"

With that, the colour drained from Sergeant Bates face, and the fear showed, he knew how nasty Wilson could be.

"By the way, don't call me by my first name, it's sir to you, understand?"

"That sounds like dissension in the ranks", Derek whispered to Jeff, "Let's go, we need to get to the Central Garden area of the Estuary to see if Michael found out if there is anyone around."

They carefully made their way to the central garden area keeping alert for any small units like the one they had nearly stumbled across by looking out for windmill vanes in the shape of a kiss instead of a cross.

=o=

"Over here it's safe." They heard Michael call softly as they approached the Central Gardens area and what was left of "The Swan" public house. It was then that Jeff noticed one or two windmills in gardens or on houses with the vanes in the shape of a kiss.

"See it works", Cyril said, pointing to the windmills as he greeted them, "by the way we had fun whilst you were away with Wilson's troops. There's not that many of them by the looks of it. We think there's only one small squad on the Island, and they look reluctant to carry out the orders Wilson is giving them, how did you get on?"

"We ran into them twice", Derek said, and excitedly told them of the incident with the trucks and how they thought they were going to shoot all the civilians and how they had humiliated the troops by disarming them and getting them to drop their trousers earlier in the day, and the recent run-in at the Cellars.

"No wonder Wilson is pissed off big time." Cyril said, "things don't seem to be going his way."

"Good", said Jen to Jeff, with a saucy smile on her face as she came out of the shadows and giving all three of them a hug, "take a load off your feet, and rest up. We have more recruits to keep an eye open for trouble. And by the way, did you notice you had a hard job getting around the debris? That's been put there to delay any troops in case they accidentally find out where we are? That was my idea."

Then she said proudly, "you walked past five of the new recruits without seeing them. Michael did better than you two, he spotted them after he passed the first two. We told the pickets to keep an eye open for you, now we'll let the other safe areas know that you're with us and safe."

"There are other safe areas?" Jeff queried.

"Yes", Jen said, "we haven't sat on our hands whilst you've been off gallivanting, we located a few structurally safe places that can house families, we have appointed someone to take control, as smaller units of people can move faster than large ones, also shared out our rations with them, so at least they can eat for a few days until we can decide what our best course of action is. We can send runners to the other safe locations in no time at all."

Jen continued, "come on, you must be hungry, we'll talk about this over something to eat and a cup of tea."

"You're well sorted out", Derek said admiringly.

"It takes a woman to get you men organized", Jen retorted laughingly.

"I'm not going down that road again", Jeff said, "the last time I had this type of conversation with you I took a good hiding."

Jen, laughed,

They sat down, ate a warm meal of rabbit stew and then drank the hot tea with no milk.

~ *0* ~

"So, what have you been up to?" Jen asked, "when they were alone, and what did you find?"

Jeff told her about the papers they had found in Councillor Randle's house, then passed her a few of the copies he had taken for her to read adding, "I haven't had time to read and digest them properly yet myself, but from the initial reading, it opens a can of worms and "Sir William" and this Wilson bloke are in it, right up to their necks, as are other Government officials who have had their pockets lined and these papers prove it.

Randle had named all the people that are involved, also it names an extreme right-wing group referred to as "The Senate" it is all in those documents. They cover the junkets they got invited to, the deals that they got a backhander from, free holidays for themselves and their families, cars, and other presents. All of it is listed. It runs into millions and once in, they were persuaded to stay in, or they had a visit from Wilson. Apparently, at one time there were four people who wanted out, but after a visit from Wilson one changed his mind, two had fatal accidents, and one apparently committed suicide.

It's all there, and it was Randle's guarantee of safety, but he obviously did not take into consideration that Wilson is a very dangerous megalomaniac. And he wanted those papers, and he snapped Randle's neck to get them, and to cover his tracks he made it look like a break-in by looters.

What Wilson didn't know, there was another compartment to the safe with access by a hidden lever at the back of the safe. He did not know the really damaging documents were there, he only got what was in the front of the safe, I only knew of the hidden compartment of Randle's Safe because the safe I had installed was the cheaper version of the same model of safe, the salesman at the time, wanted to sell me the up-graded version Randle had, and showed me the hidden compartment, but I could not afford it."

"These are copies, where are the originals?" Jen asked.

"As I said to our government friend John, safe", answered Jeff.

"You don't trust anybody, do you?" Jen commented.

"It's not that I don't trust you, it's more a case of if you don't know, you can't get killed for not knowing, I trust you with my life, and the copies of these papers, but I don't want to see all of you be heroes where Wilson is concerned. He's a killer with no scruples, that's why "Sir William" chose him."

"So, what's been happening with you lot today?" Jeff asked, just as Cyril came in the door.

Jen's face lit up when she saw Cyril, then said, "Cyril just missed being seen by a maniac driving a green Jag going towards the Terminal as he came away from there", Jen interjected.

"I thought you weren't going to take anymore risks after the last episode", Jeff said, turning to Cyril.

"There's more than one way into that Terminal without being seen, besides, what I learned from Wilson's henchmen I think is important", Cyril said.

"And if you had got caught", Jeff interjected, "I would have lost a friend, and Jen would have lost someone she loves dearly. Don't you think there's been enough killing? Remember these bastards play for keeps."

Jeff looked concerned, and said, "Promise me you won't risk your life unnecessarily." Resignedly he looked at Cyril and said "So, consider you have been told off because I care o.k.", he tried to look stern but he also smiled.

Cyril gave him a look as if to say, I hear what you say, but I am not listening, then Cyril gave him a mock rude sign with his fingers.

"Did you see what he just did", Jeff said to Jen pointing at Cyril, "I am mortified."

"Pack it in you two, you're worse than a couple of kids", Jen said.

Then Jeff turned to Cyril and said, "well what did you learn?"

Cyril looked at him like a little boy who had been told off and praised at the same time, "well, I overheard them saying that they're moving the papers from the Terminal. Also, so they don't raise any suspicions they are burning them at the mainland tip, especially as smoke coming from the Terminal will raise suspicion, but smoke coming from the Mainland tip would not look unusual."

"Who's taking these papers to the tip and when are they doing it?" Jeff asked.

"Well, from what I overheard," Cyril said, "I understand Wilson's second in command apparently, (rat-faced little man) he was getting transport from the mainland, a Jag, I think. I didn't hear that bit clearly," Cyril said, "but I thought they said to torch it as well."

Derek, who was standing by the door, he had just entered and said to Jeff, "Wasn't there a green Jag missing from Councillor Randle's underground car parking place in his back garden?"

"If they use that Jag, and the police pull them up, they might be able to tie it in with the hit and run that killed that police inspector, the mainland police will show them no mercy", Jeff said.

"What police inspector?" Cyril asked.

"It's a long story, and I'll tell you about it later", Jeff said.

Cyril added, "That's not all. When I overheard them talking, they all seemed pleased on the massive bonus they were going to receive after tomorrow. When Sir William takes over the country, he is motioning a vote of no confidence. With this vote of no confidence in the Prime Minister and the support he has, he feels certain he will win. After which he intends to install martial law using his special units of men he has in place, in all strategic places. All is then ready for him to take control of the country."

Cyril added, "I also took some photos of who was there, and of them destroying evidence of there being an accident. It was very strange, they were also making a recording, that sounded like a terrorist threat, that they were going to say they had received."

"Well, it looks like events are overtaking us", Jeff said. "There's not a lot of time to get the people that are left on the Estuary safe and the papers we have into the media before they are taken over by Sir William. Also, we must get a message out to John as soon as possible so he can nail them at his end", Jeff added.

"Drink your tea first, and then get in touch", Jen said, "you've been at it all day. We'll give you privacy if that's what you want."

"It's too late for secrets between us", Jeff said, "we've been through too much now to have secrets from one another."

He picked up the mobile phone and rang the number John had given him, he heard John's voice at the other end of the phone.

Jeff told him what they had found out between them all, and about the coup that was set for tomorrow, then asked him if he had received the fax which had been sent of the papers from Councillor Randle's house.

"Do you want me to pick your people up tonight?" John asked, "If so, how many are there? and where do you want the pick-up point to be?"

"First thing in the morning, about 8 am", Jeff said, "I'll need to get them all together. I'm not sure how many at this moment in time, but we'll be at the golf course."

"Bring the original papers with you, so we can study them", John said.

As John rang off, Jeff heard him say to someone, "yes, we have them all at last."

Jeff had a nagging feeling of doubt in the back of his mind that he could not put his finger on, but he put it down to nerves, and that all this intrigue, he was sure it would all be over soon. But he still looked puzzled.

"What's up?" Jen asked him.

He told all of them that were there about the conversation he had and then added, "I'm not sure. Things just don't ring true, but perhaps it's just me and I'm just getting nervous."

They all sat around a makeshift table, drinking tea and discussing their options and how to avoid

Wilson's men, or if the worst came to worst, it might be necessary to take them on.

A man came in that Jeff had not seen before, it was obvious he had been listening intently to the conversation, he then said, "It's not up to us to take on the professionals, we're not trained for it. We're better off out of it."

Then the man added, "If they said they would pick our people up at 8 am in the morning then that's great. We can consider it's all over and that's got to be good. All this ducking and diving will be over and we can rebuild our lives."

"This is my nephew Alan", Cyril said, "he just came in this morning to help us. He works at Scotland Yard."

Jeff eyed the man up and down. For some reason, he did not trust the man but he could not put his finger on why.

"I see you're a Doubting Thomas?" Alan said, "you don't want to believe this is over, do you?" then added, "you've been fighting the establishment for so long you don't know how to stop. You want it to carry on, don't you?"

Jeff just raised an eyebrow waiting for the arrogant man to finish, but he said nothing.

Then Alan started to goad Jeff and said, "I believe it's your only purpose in life and there's nothing else for you."

Then because he was not getting any reaction from Jeff, Alan accusingly said, "You have to have a reason for your ego trip so you can be the people's hero", he said rudely, then laughingly, he continued, then very arrogantly saying, "I for one will be glad to help clear this mess up and build us back up to normal life and get my Uncle back with his sister, she needs him and he's suffered enough."

Jeff saw red and could not control his temper anymore and flew for Alan. Derek grabbed him and held him back, "You consider that I'm on some ego trip, and what's happened here can be returned to normal?" Jeff snapped furiously.

"We have to rebuild, and rise like a phoenix out of the ashes", Alan taunted.

"The ashes of those hundreds of children, families, and all that devastation", Jeff said, "that's a price too high for me, and I believe someone should pay for that, and we should carry on fighting until the end to find the truth."

"What is the end, everybody killed?" Alan asked, "you said, according to the phone call you just had with your mysterious contact, whoever they are, that according to you we have to trust them, that they'll take us out of here, therefore we should go."

"Let's see what the others think first shall we?" Jeff asked, ignoring the retort and starting to calm down.

"Well, we need to let them know about tomorrow at the Golf Course and the meeting at 08-00 hours", Alan said, then quickly added, "so if you like, I'll go to the other locations with my uncle and tell them about the meeting."

Then Alan added slyly, "by the way, are you bringing any papers with you? If there are a lot, I can help you with them."

"No need, I can get them from their safe hiding place on my own when they're required", Jeff replied very warily.

"Don't be so touchy, I was only trying to help, that's all", Alan said, then turned to Cyril and said, "If you show me on the map where all the other groups are, we can start out now as soon as I get my stuff."

The two of them huddled together over a map of the Estuary area and then Alan left.

"Who is he?" Jeff asked Cyril.

"He's my sister's boy. He asked her if he could help us", he said, "she sent him over to us", Cyril explained, "he might be a bit hot-headed, but I'll vouch for him."

"Are you sure?" Jeff asked.

"You doubt him, you doubt me, he is family", Cyril spat out and then stormed out in a huff.

"Ok, you win", Jeff shouted after him, "I'm sorry", not wanting to make an enemy of Cyril.

They drank their tea in silence, then after a while, Jen said, "You don't seem convinced? Cyril's been with us from the start, he was shot defending what we all believe in."

"It's not that I don't trust Cyril, it's his nephew that I'm not so sure of. Perhaps I'm being a cynical old bastard", Jeff replied wryly.

"Well, you spoke to that bloke John on the phone and he's arranging it all so what are you worried about?" Jen said.

"Yeah, but I'm worried. He forgot to call me "dad" in our conversation or refer to any "tobacco" which was our password", Jeff said.

"Well, call him back using a different number if you're so worried", she said cynically, "you've upset Cyril, to let him think you don't trust him after all he's done, and all we've been through recently.

If you feel you need to check up on your information, why don't you use one of the numbers you had before to contact this John bloke?"

"Why is it women always use common sense in these situations?" Jeff mused smiling at her and took out the mobile phone. He dialled a previous number knowing he was taking a chance on being tracked and traced to this location.

After a while, John's voice answered the phone saying, "It's for me, it's my dad. I'm sorry, I told him not to call me here, I'll take it in the other room", and then Jeff heard a door close in the background.

"What the hell are you doing calling me on this phone for?" John's voice snapped, I thought I gave you a burn phone and a different number."

"You did, and I just phoned you on it, and you said you were going to pick us all up at 08-00 hours, tomorrow with all the paperwork that you wanted."

"What! I said that? When did I say that?" John asked instantly intent and alert.

"An hour and half an hour ago, it was your voice on the phone I'll swear to it", Jeff replied.

"It wasn't me," John exclaimed, "whoever it was might have used a voice replication machine, I've been in this meeting for over two hours", John explained, "did I mention our password, tobacco or my dad?"

"No," Jeff said, "that's what made me suspicious, but it sounded so like you."

"They are brilliant machines, but they are not foolproof," John explained.

Then in the silence that followed, the realization struck Jeff, "so it looks like you have a traitor in your organization", Jeff said.

"That's what this meeting has been about", John said, "We caught a traitor who has been a leak in our department for years, and he was copying those papers you sent and was sending them on to Wilson, but up till now Sir William denies any involvement."

"By the way, the man died sending the last message to Wilson, and at the moment we can't prove a direct link to Sir William yet, but we're working on it. My people are studying those copies you sent and we believe there's a link that proves that Sir William is in it right up to his neck but we need the originals to prove it, for concrete evidence, so I hope you have them somewhere safe."

"I have, but don't take too long proving that link. We're out on a limb here", Jeff said, "Also, like you, I think we might have a traitor in our midst as well.

If the shit hits the fan make your way to any army post outside the direct perimeter as I don't think the inner ones are safe," John said.

"Now you tell me. When all these people are going right near one of them at 08-00 hours ready to be rescued", Jeff said.

"What stupid person thought that one up?" John asked, "they must think electricity bill is a rock star."

"You did in your last conversation with me", said Jeff, "which I was stupid enough to tell everybody here about."

"Then Sir William and Wilson are getting desperate and you must be hurting them big time, and like you, I believe it's a trap they've set for you", John said. "At least if you know it is a trap, you might be able to avoid it."

John, continued, saying, "remember Sir William at the moment only has small private troop units with which to operate. He uses Wilson and pressures the local army pickets into doing what he wants. If they catch everybody there now with those small units, they can nip any local opposition in the bud. Also, It will stop you from getting any more information on them, then they can cover everything up and tip the delicate balance in their favour."

"You can add to that, that they count on you being soft enough and force you into giving them that paperwork if they torture or threaten to kill your new-found friends. If they get that paperwork they've won. So, they mustn't get their hands on it, no matter what it costs."

John also added, "The people they intend to trap, have to be warned. I'll do what I can on my end, but it will be a close-run thing."

John said, "I must go now or Sir William will get suspicious, and if that happens, he'll cover everything he is doing up", he added, "everything, is very finely balanced on a knife-edge and can go either way.so take care these people play for keeps."

The call with John ended. Jeff went and found Jen and asked her where Cyril and his nephew were. She told him that they'd gone to the other safe houses to get the people to meet tomorrow morning at 8 am by the golf course.

Jeff told her about the conversation he had just had with John.

Jen said, "Can you trust this second person called John that you spoke to."

"I think so", Jeff replied, "but there again my father always said to me, walk gently in this world, but carry a big stick, at the moment we have no choice as they will be crawling over the Estuary like a pack of wolves tomorrow."

Jen changed the subject and tried to ease the situation between him and Cyril,

"Cyril's nephew is an officer stationed at Scotland Yard and is on compassionate leave, as his mum, who is Cyril's sister is seriously ill. He seems well informed and certain it's over, and that the relief forces will be here tomorrow. Cyril swears by what his nephew says."

"I don't know why, but I have this feeling about tomorrow morning, that it's a trap", Jeff said, "but I can't prove it."

"Well, there's not a lot you can do tonight, as we don't know which way they went." Jen said, "Besides, we can intercept them in the morning before they get to the golf course", then she smiled and said, "Now tell me how you got on today? According to Derek, I gather you had some fun, safe breaking and nearly being caught sending copies of papers to your contact and then being chased back to here.

By the way, where are those original documents?" Jen asked, "you didn't have them on you, and I heard Cyril's nephew asking Derek and Michael about them. He seemed very anxious to see them.

When they told him, you had gone off on your own to hide them, he wanted to know where, but they couldn't or wouldn't tell him."

Jeff replied, "I believe the fewer the people that know where they are, the fewer the people that can get hurt. It's not that I don't trust you, it's because I think too highly of you to get you hurt unnecessarily", Jeff answered, but "I will tell you what's in them and how it opens up a whole can of worms and it names the people involved.

Jeff told her the names of the people named in the documents and how they were involved.

"That's a bundle of dynamite", Jen said, "no wonder they want you dead."

"Well", he continued, "apparently Councillor Randle was responsible for coordinating all the safety issues involving any 'Top Tier COMAH' sites in the area and the relative agencies such as the Health & Safety and the Environmental Agency and the Emergency services plus he was head of the local council being the Hazardous Substance Authority, plus he chaired all the council committee's and their meetings that had anything to do with the Methane terminal since Sir William brought it.

His reports were supposed to make sure all safety aspects had been taken into consideration appertaining to the surrounding community and including them in the Land Use Planning, bearing in mind the totality of effect of a worst-case scenario at the planning permission stage.

If he hid any of the dangers reported, or failed to add them into his report, or did not let one agency know there was a problem that might affect their individual reports, then on reading those reports the councillors, and planning officials, would be getting false information and be totally unaware of when making their decision, so Councillor Randle would make sure the planning permission would go through relatively smoothly.

The documents not only list the names of the people involved, but the reports that were covered up, by whom, and when. It proves that the Gas Terminal was an accident waiting to happen and it puts Sir William Waits right in the frame as there are receipts of monies paid by him to Randle and records of other payments to other officials.

Randle knew he was being investigated by some of his fellow councillors who had had him under suspicion for some time and he had told Wilson that he had this documentation to safeguard himself, but I think Wilson killed him to shut him up. It takes a professional to break a neck like that."

Jen said, "Do you mean to say in the grand scheme of things there is a process that safeguards communities from too much high fire risk industry being sited close to them?"

"Yes", Jeff said, "it came about at a meeting I attended with County councillors. At that meeting, I was insisting that the County Council Emergency Co-ordinating Committee use its powers that it held under the Civil Contingencies Act, to safeguard against a worst-case scenario disaster, as the Government does not have a safe siting policy for 'Top Tier COMAH sites'.

The County Council are ultimately responsible for search and rescue after a major incident involving massive amounts of deaths, injuries, and area's requiring evacuation in that emergency."

"So, what went wrong here?" Jen asked.

Jeff continued, "Councillor Randle hid the evidence of the worst-case scenario reports from the councillors and officers, so when they went to a public inquiry to oppose the plans they did not have the damning reports that would have won them the case, so Sir William Waits used Councillor Randle and bent all the rules and got his planning permission."

"So, if Wilson, or Sir William, gets you with all this information, and can quietly dispose of you, it stifles the information, he covers his tracks and wins, plus he then takes over the country.", Jen said, "How come he hasn't taken you out earlier?"

"Because at first, they thought I died in the explosion that took out the meeting rooms in the Estuary, then they found out somehow about my cancelled meeting that was transferred to the mainland. They then sent someone at the last moment to go into that building to try to put a stop to us, then he thought I was killed in that Building collapse, now they know otherwise, and that I survived, so they are now out to kill me at any costs.

All the time I could keep the issues in the public media they would not attack me physically. All they did was to try to discredit me, and make me out to be some sort of anarchist.

But now that the media attention has been focused on terrorism, that has all changed. They can attack me and accuse me of terrorism. Sir William wants me dead anyway they can get me. All the time they believed I was dead, I was safe. As soon as they found out I'm alive and with enough evidence to hang them, my life's not worth a plugged nickel, and they will do anything or use anybody to get to me."

Jeff added, "The meeting at the Estuary golf course worries me. It's too slick, and I think it's a trap."

"Well, we can't do anything tonight. You get some sleep. There are enough people on watch out there that you did not see on your way in, that will warn us. I will try to intercept the others and warn them in the morning", Jen said soothingly.

"You believe it's a trap as well?" Jeff asked.

"I'm not sure, but like you say something doesn't ring true, but I don't know what it is, so I will give it the benefit of the doubt for now. Have some bread and cheese, a cup of tea and sleep on it and sort it out in the morning", Jen said.

Jeff took a chunk of cheese, a doorstep of bread, and a mug of tea, found himself a corner to settle down in, to contemplate what to make of all that had happened in the last few days and how desperate their situation was getting. He fell asleep mulling over the problems.

Jeff woke with a start. It was still dark outside but it was what he called the fisherman's false dawn. Dawn was a while from starting to break but there was enough light for fishermen to tackle up by. He was instantly alert to his surroundings and saw men, women and children asleep all around him. He assumed that all of them had come into the shelter overnight, but none of them had disturbed him.

A little boy was looking at Jeff wide-eyed from behind his sleeping mother and whispered, "You're our leader, aren't you? You're going to save us all from the bad men. My mum said I wasn't to wake you up, I didn't, did I?"

"No," Jeff said soothingly to the little boy.

At that moment, the little boy's mother woke up and told the little boy off for disturbing him in harsh whispers.

"He didn't, I was awake anyway", Jeff said, attempting to stop the child from being reprimanded anymore.

The boy looked pleased with himself that he had been vindicated and said, "Did you really shoot that helicopter down and shoot the man who killed my sister?"

"Jason," his mother said, "you must not ask such rude questions to the nice man like that."

"Well did you?" the boy asked, looking at him from wide and beguiling eyes.

"Well, if you mean the man who was in the helicopter who shot a young lady who was with a young man near the Cellars, yes, I did."

"I hope he died horribly", the little boy said, "the words shocking from such a young mouth.

"Jason," his mother said again, and then she turned to Jeff, "I'm sorry", she said to him, "we've been through a lot just lately and we'll be glad for it all to be over, but let me thank you for putting that animal away for good. We won't forget it and if it's any consolation my husband would have done the same if he had lived. He worked at the Terminal and died in the explosion. Even though he worked there, he admired what you did, and the principles that you stood by, not many men have those principles and your code of ethics today."

Jeff felt embarrassed by her praise, knowing that she had lost everything and would have to struggle to bring up her children, and he said he was sorry for her loss, and that he had to get things sorted and hurried outside to look around.

"You're an early bird, a voice announced behind him."

It was Cyril, "Sorry I went off in a huff last night, damned pride", he said, "Alan and I have always been close, but he gets headstrong sometimes and can only think of what suits him like most youngsters today. But I put him straight.

I sent him off to bring in the out-posts so we can all get everyone together and all meet up at the same time at the golf course, but I understand from Jen you have reservations about your first message and about us all going there? Do you think it's a trap?"

"Yes", Jeff answered, "but I can't put my finger on it, things just don't ring true."

"Well, I'll take the people there and if it is a trap, we'll be prepared for it," Cyril replied, then said, "you do what you do best, that's follow the evidence."

"By the way! I heard the papers that were in the Terminal Control Room are being moved to the Tip this morning for burning by Wilson's second in command in that green Jag." Cyril added, "you can cut him off if you go via the North Creek crossing to the tip. He has to go all the way round via the mainland as he can only use the main road and he has to go through all the debris and the roadblocks if your quick you can get there before him."

Cyril added, "I suggest you use the pushbike you used to get here on the day we met that is still by the old concrete bunker at North Corner, I think there is a couple more there as well. I'll get Derek to go with you, he's a good man to have in a tight corner, by the way, I have been talking to Jen, I now know how important this information is, so I hope all that paperwork nails those bastards once and for all."

"How did you know about those papers being moved this morning?", Jeff asked curiously.

"Alan said he overheard it when we went back to the Cellars to pick any stragglers", Cyril replied, "he said Wilson had instructed the man to burn it at the Council Tip as a fire there would raise less suspicion than a fire at the Terminal, which makes sense, Alan also said, Wilson had mentioned that he would give the man the authorisation for him to get through the roadblocks and to use the Jag to take it there as it would be easier to get a car through the picket lines than a lorry when he got to the tip, he was to burn the whole lot, Jag as well."

"Well, you're right, we must stop those papers from being burned if we can, they might be the final nail in those bastards' coffin", Jeff said, "I'll take Derek and see when we can get moving."

Jeff turned to Cyril and said, "I might not see you until sometime later, so good luck. And I hope you, Jen and the people make it safely out of here, don't forget to stay together as a group; don't let them split any of you up as you have strength in numbers. Let everybody know what's happened here. Let as many people know as possible so it can't be covered up. It might be a good idea to share out the copies of some of the documents that I gave to Jen so everybody can have one page to hide and carry that way at least some copies might be saved", then with a final goodbye, he left.

Jeff found Derek packing supplies in a knapsack, "I'm ready when you are", Jeff said to him.

"I want to say my goodbyes to Jen first," Derek said "before we go. I'll catch you up, where will you be?" Derek asked.

I'll make my way to the North Corner, passing near to where I lived, I'll pick up something from there on my way passed", Jeff said and started to make his way to his bungalow, making use of the natural cover, looking behind him watching as all the people started gathering together to make their way to the Estuary golf course.

He carefully made his way. The area was undisturbed just as it had been since he last left it, Jeff made his way to his safe, opened it, retrieved the papers he had put in the safe and checked to see if they were all there, put them in his inside jacket pocket and started to leave.

A voice said, "I'll have those."

Jeff spun round to face Alan, Cyril's nephew, who was holding a gun aimed at his chest.

"Very clever, hiding the documents we've been looking for in a place we had already searched. We never thought of that", Alan said.

Alan added, "I knew we could flush you out, if we drip-fed you the information, and let you know about moving those papers from the Gas Terminal that Uncle Cyril found out about, Oh! It is true they are being moved and being burnt at the tip today, we can't risk them being exposed, so we used the information to catch you, you don't know how much of a pain you have been."

"I never trusted you, but Cyril will kill you for betraying everyone like this", Jeff said, raising his hands slowly.

"He'll never find out." Alan said, "he and the rest of them pilgrims are being rounded up as we speak and they'll be in a concentration camp for many years as suspected terrorists. Anyway, if he did find out it was me, I'll be long gone, and spending the £2 million pounds I get for you and these papers from Sir William."

Alan moved in very threateningly, and said, "I've been itching to take you out, ever since you got me demoted a few years ago when one of your swampy mates had an accident and got killed in my custody. They didn't really believe he fell down the stairs trying to escape."

Jeff remembered the death in custody of his friend Doug only too well, and the "hue and cry" that went on at the time.

"Those stairs you mentioned Doug died on, only led down to the cells, so how could he have been escaping and in handcuffs?" Jeff retorted.

"I can tell you now as you won't be around to repeat it", Alan explained very menacingly, "he had the IQ of an ice cube, and he wouldn't tell me what I wanted to know about who was going to be at that demonstration? So maybe I did hit him harder than I should have, it was his fault. If he had listened in the first place, and told me who the others were, he wouldn't have died."

Then Alan added, "I tried to get you and missed you when that building on the mainland collapsed, I was spotted by that government agent, he thought I was on his side until he stepped in front of me, his death was very quick. he did not know I was trying to get those papers with the list of names from your friend Bob way back then. We knew then if you and Bob married up the names on those lists it was only a matter of time and we would have been exposed and we could not risk that.

We thought we had the list when we got Bob's case, we did not know Bob had given you his copy of the list until it was too late and then faxes of documents from Councillor Randle's safe started turning up at HQ, which threatened to expose everything."

Jeff looked at Alan, he was holding the gun in his left hand, then he remembered what John's man was looking for, a left-hander or as he had said, A southpaw.

Alan continued boasting, "Now it is going to be chalked up to terrorists and Sir William gets control of the country and I retire in luxury."

"So, if people don't do what you want, they die?" Jeff said, "then you, Wilson and Sir William make good bedfellows. I have not known your uncle for long but I do know your Uncle Cyril would kill you if he knew what you were really like."

"He's not likely to find out with you dead, him interned and me living the life of luxury I've always dreamed of", Alan said confidently, "Sir William helped me out when your friend Doug died, he covered for me then, and paid for an expensive brief so no charges were brought, but I still got demoted and that you will pay for, and with the reward on your head, dead or alive, I can retire to a villa in Spain."

Then he added, "I always believed revenge is best served cold, it's so much sweeter, and boy is this going to be sweet."

Jeff's mind was racing. What could he do against what appeared to be a professional killer? Then he had an idea, on a wild guess asked, "Your last name is Wild, isn't it? I read that name recently, I know, it's in some of those documents that Sir William wants so badly, now I'm curious as to what you're going to do with the documents of Councillor Randle's that name you."

"What documents name me? Where are they?" Alan asked, suddenly uncertain.

"Some of these documents", Jeff said pointing to the safe, "or are you going to let Sir William have them? then he can have a bigger hold over you than he has now."

Alan looked confused as to what to do at that moment, and then he said, "I don't have time to look through all those papers and pick out the ones that affect me, so if you show me the right papers I'll make your death clean if not, it's going to be very painful. Remember, I've killed before so no funny stuff."

Alan added, "Remember, I know where to hurt with or without it showing and don't forget you've been registered as dying at the Center in the explosion so you've been living on borrowed time, and that time has ended now."

Alan moved slowly towards Jeff still holding the gun levelled at Jeff's chest, "let me have the relative documents and be quick about it."

"I need to find them first", Jeff said, making out that he was rummaging around in the safe, he was trying to play for time.

"Come on, don't mess me about", Alan said, firing a shot at him. It ricocheted off the ground near to where Jeff was standing.

"Ok, give me a chance to find the right pages", Jeff said hurriedly, "you want all of them, don't you?"

"Yes, but be quick about it and stop stalling for time", Alan said knowingly.

Jeff's mind was doing overtime, trying to figure out how he could jump on Alan and catch him unaware but Alan was keeping a safe distance away from him. He would have to get him closer to stand a fighting chance of surprising him.

"Here are two of them", Jeff said holding up two pages, "and there are some more pages with your name on them."

"Let's have them then", Alan said.

Jeff moved towards him, ready to spring at him when he had the chance.

"That's far enough", Alan said, "you can put them down on the ground where you are and move back to the safe and carry on looking for more documents with my name on them."

Alan picked up the papers and started reading them, at the same time flicking his eyes towards Jeff keeping a watchful eye on Jeff and on what he was doing.

Alan whistled and said, "Councillor Randle, had us all by the short and curlies, didn't he, anymore, like these there?"

"I think so", Jeff said, "I'll look."

After a few minutes, Alan began getting impatient, and said, "I am not waiting much longer, come on get a move on, are there anymore or not?"

"Yes, here", said Jeff, holding out a bundle of papers.

"Let's have them now", Alan said, moving towards him.

Jeff held out the papers, pretended to stumble on the rubble, then leapt at Alan throwing the papers in his face, and grabbing for the gun as it went off.

He felt a burning sensation in his ribs but managed to hold on to the hand holding the gun as he struggled with Alan.

Alan was much younger and much fitter than Jeff was. All Jeff had was the distant memories of when he had done judo many years ago when he was a member of the Bank's judo team so he tried a judo throw in the hope it would come off, and to his surprise it did.

Alan was shocked, as he went tumbling through the air and landed heavily, the gun flying out of his hand. He got up on his knees and said, "I didn't expect that from an old fart like you."

The gun lay on the ground near Jeff, but as he reached for it, Alan grabbed a rock and threw it at Jeff hitting him on the head.

Jeff went down stunned.

As his head was clearing, he could just make out Alan standing near him pointing the gun at him saying, "I won't underestimate you again. It's time to meet your maker", as Alan pointed the gun at him, Jeff heard three shots but there was no pain.

Then Alan collapsed in a heap in front of him.

Jeff struggled to his feet and was stunned to see Derek holding a smoking gun. "I didn't trust him either", he said.

Jeff said, "Thank Christ you turned up when you did, I thought I was a goner."

"Jen told me to look after you. I promised her I would and I don't break my promises", the big man smiled, "the only thing is he got me too", and Derek collapsed with blood pumping from a wound in his shoulder.

Jeff ripped off his own shirt and wrapped it around the wound in Derek's shoulder.

"That smarts", Derek murmured in pain, as Jeff used Derek's coat as a sling.

Derek asked, "How is our friend?"

"He's gone off", Jeff replied.

"That bastard went off years ago from what I hear", Derek said.

"How are you feeling now?" Jeff asked, being very concerned, then added, "by the way what made you follow me here?"

"It was Michael's idea," Derek said. "He's got a lot more upstairs than people give him credit for. If you think no-one knew where you were hiding your paperwork, he knew from day one, but he didn't tell anyone and when he saw Alan was missing, he was suspicious. He told me to check here first. Just as well. When I heard that first shot, I thought I was too late, but I just made it, I knew that little shit had it in for you ever since he turned up out of the blue, but Cyril wouldn't have a word said against him."

"All I can say is thanks", Jeff said, "I owe you my life and I won't forget it."

"Well it's no good sitting here", Derek said, "We must get those other papers from Wilson's second in command at the tip if we are going to nail them all. It's too late to warn Jen and Cyril, all we can hope for is if they heard those shots and that might alert them."

"Before you go anywhere", Jeff said, "I need to see that wound. It looks clean, and I think it missed the bone", then Jeff jokingly said, "we don't need you bleeding all over creation just to get some sympathy from Jen."

Derek blushed, and said, "Does it show that I think a lot of that girl?"

"Just a bit", Jeff said, "but I won't tell anybody", and then winced as he moved because his ribs were starting to hurt. He looked down at his ribs to see a large bruise forming and a wound at his side where the bullet went through.

"Not a very good shot, was he?" Derek said, "you're not exactly a small target, are you?" looking at Jeff's wound.

"Look who's talking you great lummox", Jeff replied.

Then they both started laughing at each other.

"Ouch, that smarts", they both said together, then laughed again.

"He couldn't hit a barn door at ten paces", Derek said, "I winged him with the first shot, now that got his attention. Then he fired at me, hit me in the shoulder at the same time as I got him again with the second shot. This time he went down for good. Bloody amateurs, they pay peanuts they get monkey's fancy sending a boy to do a man's job, what do they expect." Derek retorted.

Derek's shoulder was a clean flesh wound and not as serious as it looked.

Jeff's wound looked ugly but not life-threatening. He thought he had a few broken ribs where the bullet had glanced of his ribs.

They patched one another up with the cloth left from their shirts, put their jumpers back on and then their coats.

"Come on, we have a few things to do and place to be in no time at all", Derek said, "can't sit here all day sunning ourselves." Pulling Jeff to his feet gently he said, "We need to find those bikes, I hope some tea leaf hasn't nicked them."

They both laughed,

Jeff winced and said, "Stop making me laugh, it hurts my ribs", but this remark just made them laugh even more.

"What do we do with him?" Derek asked, pointing at the crumpled body of Cyril's nephew.

"Let him rot. Worms have got to eat", Jeff said, "he would have let you rot if he'd had his way. I tell you what, if we see Cyril, we'll let him know, and then if he wants to, he can claim the body."

They made their way to North Corner to find the bikes so they could cycle to the tip via the Creek barrier then onto the council mainland tip.

They found the bikes hidden behind the concrete bunker and made their way down North Road to Creek barrier.

"I'll go ahead", Jeff said, "just in case, it might be safer."

He cycled along silently and got to the barrier. It seemed as though nobody was around. Then he spotted a very young policeman lying dozing in the morning sun.

As he approached, the young policeman woke up startled "Who are you? And where did you come from? are you my relief? I've been here since yesterday with no break." Then with a realisation spotted Jeff wounds, "Hey, you're wounded", he said, "How that happened?"

Jeff pretended to be very hurt and staggered off his bike towards the young policeman.

You look bad, the policeman said, just as Jeff sprang into action and hit him hard. The policeman went down, out cold.

"Not a bad right hook", Derek said as he approached, then added, "I must remember that."

They made there way across the barrier, and then on towards the Tip without a major incident, or being seen, they managed to dodge two of Wilson's trooper patrols on the way by ducking down behind a hedge.

They got to the tip. But it seemed closed and the gates looked locked.

As they waited by a closed gate for the green Jag to turn up, they looked at each other's wounds checking to see if they had got worse.

They heard a car engine being gunned, and sure enough, the green Jag was approaching.

"Leave this to me", Derek said, "he knows you. Hide behind the concrete pillar so you're not seen."

The Jag pulled up and a man got out and started opening the gate. As he was doing so, he spotted Derek.

"What are you doing here?" the man asked, in a tense voice.

"Finding bits for a shelter", Derek replied.

"Well clear off, you're not allowed near here", the man said.

"I got family, we've got to survive", Derek said trying to look destitute with a pleading look, "and anyway, who says I'm not allowed here?"

"Find bits for your shelter somewhere else", the man ordered harshly.

"All right mister. Just trying to survive", Derek said, edging his way closer to the man.

"That's far enough", the man said, then he pulled out a gun and threatening Derek with it.

Then seeing Derek's bleeding wound, he said "You've been shot. You're wanted by the troopers, move away from me or I'll give you another bullet, this time where it hurts."

It was then that Jeff moved out from behind the pillar pointing his gun at the man and said, "Put your gun down nice and slowly."

The man spun around and faced Jeff.

"You! I was told you were dead", The man said recognising Jeff straight away.

Jeff added, "Look, we're not after you, just the papers in the car, so don't be a hero for a shit like Wilson, he's not worth it."

The man thought about it and then handed the gun to Derek.

"What am I going to say to Wilson?" the man asked.

"Tell him we jumped you, knocked you out, and stole the car", Jeff said.

"And how and when did this happen?" the man queried.

"Just now, like this", Derek said, landing the man a roundhouse that pole-axed him and laid him flat.

Derek, then said, "he was in two minds, simple, and dim, and he talked too much, Ouch, that smarts", holding his shoulder.

"If you've opened that wound again, I'll have words with you", Jeff joked. He then approached Derek and checked his shoulder, looking quite concerned. "You're bleeding like a stuck pig, why did you have to hit him so hard?"

"I only tapped him", Derek said putting on an innocent look.

"Well I don't want one of your taps", Jeff said, looking concerned, then added, "we need to get you medical attention urgently, you're losing a lot of blood."

Derek said, "No, you'll get caught then all this will have been for nothing, and besides, I promised Jen I would look out for you."

"You have, and you are", Jeff said trying to appease the big man, "but even massive tanks like you run out of petrol sometimes, come on, we'll use the car to get you to a medical unit."

They got into the Jaguar, turned it around and with Jeff driving, drove back in the direction the man had just come from.

Jeff spotted a wrench that was tucked down beside his seat.

After a mile or two they came across a sentry post.

Jeff reached for the wrench that he found.

They approached the sentry post slowly. As they got level with the hut, the trooper came out looking very bored, "You weren't long", he said, then quickly realised that it was a different person driving the car than the one he was instructed to let into the tip and had expected to walk out after destroying the car and everything in it. Whilst the trooper was puzzling at this Jeff swung the wrench, hitting the trooper on the side of the head. He went down in a heap and they sped off before anyone could react.

After a short while, they turned a corner and there in front of them in the distance was a roadblock with troopers stationed at strategic points along with it.

"Let me drive and you make a run for it", Derek said.

"They've seen us. If we don't go towards them, they'll open fire", Jeff said, "We'll try to bluff our way through."

"Let me drive", Derek said again, "if it comes to it, I can't run very far with this wound and you stand a better chance then I do of getting through. Also, I can draw them off using the car but we must get passed this checkpoint first".

As they swapped seats, Derek asked, "Have you got the most important papers on you?"

Jeff tapped his inside pockets, then said, "try to save this lot as well, if you can, you ready?"

"As ready as I'll ever be", Derek said, moving the car forward smoothly.

As they approached the checkpoint, a trooper lazily approached the car. By the time he realised that it was not the driver he had let through a little while ago, it was too late.

Derek hit the accelerator and gunned the Jaguar into the checkpoint, barging his way past the trooper and bursting his way through the checkpoint. They went speeding down the road with the troopers opening fire at them as they went around the corner.

"It was lucky they were fast asleep", Derek said with some satisfaction.

"Not for long", Jeff said as he looked into the wing mirror and saw troopers running for a jeep and starting to give chase.

"We won't be so lucky next time, not with them on our tail. It's time we split up, one or both of us must try to get through to your mate John, with some of the papers we have between us", Derek said, "I suggest you bail out before the next roadblock and try to make it on foot. I'll lead them a merry dance away from you, which will give you a fighting chance."

"What about you?" Jeff asked, not liking the idea at all.

"I can't move very fast with this", Derek said pointing at his chest that was starting to bleed profusely. I won't get very far on foot. I'll only hold you up. It's a pity I didn't know you earlier, we could have been life-long friends." With that Derek slowed the car down just as they were turning a right-hand corner and pushed Jeff out of the car.

Jeff rolled into some bushes, and the Jaguar with Derek in it sped off leaving Jeff in a heap hidden from the road by the bushes.

The Jeep with the troopers in came past at quite a speed but they failed to see him and carried on down the road after the speeding Jaguar.

All Jeff could do was to mentally wish the big man luck.

==o==

Jeff climbed up the slope to the top of the hill of the well-known landmark which overlooked the whole of the lower Estuary.

Jeff checked his surroundings. He could see from where he stood that on the hill in the distance there were makeshift tents and shelters and he made his way towards them hoping to hide in amongst the survivors and refugees of the disaster that were setting up the shanty type shelters.

Cutting across fields and hugging the hedgerows to avoid being seen by any patrols he made his way slowly towards the hill and towards the first group of makeshift tin huts and plastic sheet covered shelters.

He was met with suspicion and resentment by the survivors, so he moved slowly on across the small encampment trying to look as inconspicuous as possible. He was aware of receiving suspicious glances when the people saw the make-shift blood-covered bandages and the steady flow of blood running down his side.

He made his way from one small encampment to another slowly, trying to blend in, but unbeknown to him he was being watched by a trooper in an observation post. The trooper phoned into his section leader what he had seen, and said he wanted to claim the reward for spotting Jeff.

The section leader, in turn, contacted Wilson telling him, his man had spotted Jeff, and where he was last seen.

Wilson said, "Great news, at last, we have got him", Wilson mobilised two squads immediately. Both squads to surround the area and carry out a search plus a small fast response unit was sent to the location indicated by the observation post. He also ordered his helicopter to pick him up and take him to the location.

As he was waiting for his helicopter, he phoned Sir William Waits, but there was no answer from Sir William's phone, so he left a message telling Sir William that Jeff had been spotted near the makeshift shelters and he had him cornered. Wilson also told Sir William when he had Jeff, he was going to show him no mercy, and enjoy questioning him intently then kill him slowly.

As he heard his helicopter approaching to pick him up, he went into graphic details over the phone as to what he was going to do to Jeff and he was going to enjoy it. He spoke in great detail how he was going kill him slowly and get all and any incriminating papers he was carrying then and burn them.

Wilson came out of his revelry and had to ring off quickly as his helicopter was ready and he was eager to teach Jeff a lesson about how not to mess with him. He picked up his gun on the way out of the door, checking for the knife he had hidden in the sleeve of his sock.

There were make-shift tents and shelters made from any scrap that could be scrounged or purloined with bare hands, and people walked around this threadbare settlement looking dazed and desperate.

Jeff crumpled to his knees, nearly broke down and cried. As he surveyed the devastation, the memory now etched in his mind which he had tried to forget, now flooded to the forefront of his mind. The vision of the school with the horror of the little ones, now it hit him hard, from his vantage point, he could see the totality of the disaster. Why did the Authorities not listen? He said to himself, he sobbed bitterly and heart brokenly, it suddenly hit him as he came to terms with the loss and horror of the total devastation he could see.

With the desperation of survival and the pain from his wound threatening to overwhelm him, he mentally forced himself to get up off his knees and struggle on.

Over this short period of time, he had had to make his way from one pitiful, crowded survivors camp to another. The bare fact that he had survived was of no consolation, as nearly everything that was a vibrant community had been wiped out, gone, no more, in the total devastation which had occurred.

He did not want to be here, in this place, at this time, a mental and physical witness to the anguish, loss of hope and stunned disbelief which permeated the air about him like a heavy veil of fog, but he had to see it through. So many were now relying on him. With Alan dead, he knew Wilson, would not be far behind, so he was now being hunted by another desperate professional killer who would stop at nothing to see him dead.

As he looked around as to what had been one of the most crowded and expensive areas to live in, this part of the country was now a wasteland, as far as the eye could see. People who had survived, who had once been very wealthy, now stood with only rags on their backs, the only possessions they had left. Ironically, their money which had once bought nice houses, nice clothes, and holidays had not, when it came down to it, bought life.

The devastation that lay before and around him was unbelievable. From where he stood he could see the Hiroshima-type explosion had totally destroyed and wiped out the whole of the Estuary industry, killing thousands of people, crippling the country's economy and brought the Government to its knees. It had put the structure of life in this part of the country back to the dark ages.

He looked across at the devastating scene before him. It was like looking at a scene where someone had been allowed to go berserk with a giant blowtorch.

Many of the trees had had their branches shrivelled into charcoal. The bark of the trunks and large branches being black and charred. In some places, the ground had been seared black. A bitter acrid smell permeated the air.

In other places, it looked as though the area had hardly been touched by the conflagration. Some houses still remained standing but there were no windows or doors. Some houses looked as though a mighty foot had trodden on them, other buildings were partially collapsed whilst others had been reduced to a pile of rubble.

Where there had once been a very busy, complex, thriving industry on the Estuary area, there was now a mangled mass of metal and twisted, drunken looking buildings. It was a panoramic scene of unbelievable devastation that seemed impossible for him to comprehend, and it would be seared in his memory forever.

As Jeff looked at what seemed to be a war-torn vista, it seemed unbelievable that any life could and did exist within its vicinity.

It had taken Jeff nearly an hour from when Derek had sped off to arrive at where he was now standing and he was getting weaker with the loss of blood and the pain from his wound.

He realised with a start that it had only been a few days since he had left the Police Sergeant who he only knew as Dick, and the Government man named John, in the mainland Police station.

Worst of all, he now had to live with the fact that he had been the cause that killed someone, though he felt that the man had more than deserved it.

He was now being hunted by Wilson and his men like some prized animal. It was a human safari, and he was the prey they were after. All Jeff wanted to do was survive, hopefully, long enough to reach the Government man named John, and reveal the evidence he had. That was his only option now.

As Jeff was making his way from one small refugee camp to another, he got to the brow of the little hill. It was then he spotted the first lot of troopers heading his way.

He knew he was being hunted by professional people who had no other intention but to kill him quietly at their first opportunity. According to them, he had to be shut up at all costs, and the evidence he had against them and their boss, had to be destroyed.

His thoughts were disrupted as he heard the throb of a helicopter engine and the thrum of the rotor blades. He hoped that it wasn't getting too close.

Jeff forced himself to stride with a disguised, easy pace, to give the impression he was not wounded or weakening. Hoping he would blend in, he passed by a large tent and saw on the other side of the slope the group of men in line dressed in black military-style uniform heading his way. He promptly backtracked to the other side of the temporary refugee town only to see another group of men attired in the same type of uniform also heading his way, cutting off his retreat. He could now see that he was being hemmed in on two sides. Jeff knew without a doubt that he had been spotted, and the men dressed in black were searching for him.

It was then that a helicopter flew high over the tree stumps and denuded vegetation and swept down to where he had hastily hidden amongst a pile of blackened and splintered wreckage of a farm building.

Out of desperation he gave one last effort rather than be caught like a rat in a trap, and made a dash over the uneven ground for a small copse of trees. As he ran, his side where he had been wounded began to cause him pain, and he realised that he was getting very short of breath and started to stagger.

Out of the corner of his eye, he saw puffs of ash and dust begin to spurt from the ground and round and about his running feet and he realised that it was caused by the ricocheting of bullets which were being spat at him from a high calibre gun set on automatic by someone in the helicopter.

He made it to the copse of trees. The helicopter had to sweep high over the trees to avoid hitting the top branches. In his haste, Jeff ran straight into a group of soldiers who were brewing up tea, which was part of a much larger unit.

Jeff was promptly and unceremoniously pinned to the ground by two soldiers whilst their colleagues formed a group around them, and in turn, the soldiers started returning fire at the helicopter as did the rest of the alerted squad.

Bullets could be heard ricocheting off the body of the helicopter. The rotor blades stuttered and attempted to carry on revolving, the engine coughed and spluttered, and then the whole contraption came down in a cloud of smoke and impacted with the ground hard.

As the helicopter slammed to the ground the pilot and his two passengers bailed out rolling into a fighting stance then approached the squad of soldiers with guns drawn and pointed their guns menacingly at Jeff.

Whilst they looked stunned that they had been shot down by the squad of soldiers, a man who seemed to be the leader of these troopers dressed in black was very angry as he moved smoothly towards the squad of soldiers with his gun drawn menacingly. It was Wilson and he was ready to fire his gun and kill Jeff.

The Sargent bellowed a command. The squad of soldiers swiftly closed ranks around Jeff with weapons loaded and pointing towards the crew of the helicopter. There was a distinct clicking sound as the rest of the squad of soldiers quickly formed up to support their mates, in turn, they also released the safety catches on their weapons and faced the three men who had just tumbled out of the helicopter.

"Who is in charge here?" One of the three men from the helicopter demanded as he took off his flying helmet and addressed the squad of soldiers.

Jeff's heart sank. From the description he had from Cyril, there was no doubt it was Wilson, and Wilson wanted him dead and right now. He could see that by the cold hate in the man's eyes.

"I am, and who the hell are you? And what do you mean by firing on me and my men?" came a voice from the back of the rank of soldiers. An officer appeared it seemed out of nowhere and took a wary pace forward.

Wilson, with an attempt at a more conciliatory tone, replied, "We're chasing a known leader of a terrorist organisation responsible for all this devastation, and you have him there, pinned on the ground", pointing at Jeff.

"I want him", Wilson demanded, "so hand him over, and hand him over now!"

"I said, who the hell do you think you are?" the officer repeated this time you could hear the anger in the officer's tone, "what do you mean by shooting up the area that I'm in charge of, endangering my men like you were a puny punk actor in some second rate movie."

"I want that man", Wilson said ignoring the Officer.

"I said who the hell are you?" the officer repeated, "and if you don't answer me now, you and your lot are under arrest until I can get to the bottom of this, so name and number young man, now!"

"Ray Wilson, Head of Security for Sir William Waits, and your new political head of the country", Wilson explained diffidently.

"He's not my dictator! Or the head of my country. I answer only to military orders, and you don't have any", the officer said,

"You will hand over your prisoner to me", Wilson demanded, "he is a terrorist and a threat to the country. He has personally murdered at least once and caused thousands of deaths through his activities. I believe I outrank you", Wilson went on to say, "so you will do as I tell you, and maybe" he added very arrogantly, "I won't have you charged for shooting down my helicopter."

"Who the hell do you think you are?" the officer repeated, "no civilian outranks me or my men when martial law has been imposed, you might be some sort of detective, or agent, but as far as I'm concerned you would need a search party to find your own backside, now what do you mean by attacking me and my squad, shooting at civilians, and stupidly making demands from the military?"

"I want him", Wilson said, pointing at Jeff, "so hand him over now, and remember I have people in powerful places, so you better do as I say!"

"You don't threaten the Queen's soldiers no matter who you are without taking the consequences, no matter who you're supposed to know, not if you want to stay in one piece", the officer said, "so now put your guns down, you're risking being placed under arrest by force if necessary."

"I will have your rank and see you in the guardhouse for life for this", Wilson bluffed in a threatening tone to the officer, knowing he was losing the argument.

"Whatever", the officer challenged, "I've heard pigs fart before", the officer replied to Wilson, "now I've had enough of this backwards and forwards riposte, you're under arrest until I get to the bottom of this."

Just then, there was the sound of engine's revving up the hill, a small unit of troopers turned up in trucks combined of two squads of men in black uniforms. They jumped off the trucks and approached the group of soldiers with guns drawn.

"Now this might change things", Wilson said who was now smirking to the officer, "I think the boot on the other foot now, don't you?"

The officer's face turned cold, and he bellowed in a parade ground voice, "Squad, fix bayonets, skirmishers ready! Stand by to repel borders."

The soldiers obeyed speedily and without question and fanned out into a military skirmishing line to affect the best firepower, ready for the order to fire, in the silence that followed you could hear the clicking of the safety catches coming off the rest of the squad's guns as they prepared to open fire on Wilson and his troopers.

It was a stand-off, in the tense atmosphere, you could cut the air with a knife.

"That's far enough", the officer said to the men in black, "if you come any nearer, I will order my men to open fire" and turning to Wilson stated, "you'll have a bloodbath on your hands", and then looking Wilson in the eyes, "they'll win as they are seasoned soldiers and you are not."

The men in black looked fearfully towards Wilson, uncertain of what to do. They did not sign-up to get killed fighting seasoned troops. They all looked to Wilson for instructions, it was very clear they had no stomach for a fight against seasoned troops.

"All right men", Wilson said trying to save face, and pointing at Jeff said, "he's not going anywhere now, go back to unit headquarters" and then boastingly said, "by the time I finish with this officer he'll be peeling spuds for years."

"Take him away Corporal", the officer said pointing to Wilson, "and Sergeant, have the rest of his troops disarmed and arrest them as well."

"You can't do that", Wilson said to the officer, "I will have you nailed to the wall for this."

"Threatening an officer of the Queen's Forces will get you nowhere, now you have a choice, the easy way or the hard way, and I don't mind which you choose. You can go very quietly with my men or you will be hog-tied and carried, and if any of your men interfere they will be shot, do I make myself clear", then shouting at Wilson said, "well do I?" also letting the troopers know he meant business.

"Crystal clear", Wilson said his head dropped, his bluffing did not work, so resigning himself to the situation, he had to come up with another idea.

The soldiers moved in and took Wilson away.

The rest rounded up the troopers who gave up their guns and the stand-off was over.

The expression on Wilson's face was a picture to Jeff and one that would remain in his memory offering a small sense of achievement and satisfaction for some time to come.

The men in the black uniforms who had laid down their guns were rounded up and led away to the accompaniment of sullen mutterings and vindictive glances back at the soldiers.

"Right let him up", the officer ordered pointing to the two soldiers sill pinning Jeff to the ground.

"What's this all about?" he asked Jeff, then saw Jeff was wounded.

"How did you get that?" The officer pointed to the bright red blood on Jeff's side.

"Him and his cronies", Jeff replied, wearily gesturing to Wilson as he was being led away still arguing with the squad of soldiers.

Just then a Sergeant stepped up in front of Jeff with his back towards Jeff and faced the officer.

"Yes, Sergeant?" The Officer said.

"I believe that man calling himself Wilson is not telling the truth, Sir", the Sergeant offered.

"And what do you know about this Sergeant?"

"If it helps, Quite a bit, Sir."

"It comes to something when sergeants know more than their officers", he muttered, "but there again, if the truth were known they always did."

"Well", the officer added, "God gave us two eyes, two ears, and one mouth, so we should look and listen twice as much as we shout, you had better come to my quarters now and explain yourself, and bring him with you", pointing to Jeff, "and by the way you had better get the MO to fix him up, he's bleeding like a stuck pig. We can't have him making a mess and bleeding all over my nice new quarters now, can we?"

The officer turned and marched off.

The Sergeant turned to face Jeff, and Jeff recognised him straight away as the soldier named John who had helped him out of the building after it had collapsed, sent him to the First Aid unit, that had been when this present pantomime of events had started.

"You're a sight for sore eyes, how come you're here and how's that nurse of yours?" Jeff asked with a smile, then added, "she thinks a lot of you, you know."

"We're on picket duty in this area and are moving onto the Estuary later today as part of some rescue package, Jane and I, well we're getting married when this is all over, now I got my promotion", the Sergeant pointed to the three chevron strips on his sleeve.

"How come, you're here being shot at by that maniac?" The sergeant asked, "the last time I saw you, it was miles away by headquarters, and if I remember right, I recommended first aid then as well, looks like you're going to need some more. What have you been up to?"

"I've been on walkabout since then", said Jeff wryly.

"If it's any consolation", the Sargent continued, "I know you're no more a terrorist than I am, and I know a bit more than you realise. You see my nurse and a particular police sergeant's lady friend are related, and sisters talk, small world eh."

Jeff's eyes opened with surprise, "well you could knock me down with a feather", and then said, "it certainly is a small world, isn't it?"

The Sargent said, "my officer is of the old school, very fair, but with discipline. you know where you stand with him. He'll get to the bottom of this, so let's not keep him or the MO waiting, you look as though you've been dragged through a hedge backwards, mind you not so dusty as the last time I saw you, eh", they laughed together.

As they got to the officer's quarters the soldier said, "At least I might be able to put a good word in for you, that Wilson bloke looks a nasty bit of work."

"He is", Jeff agreed firmly, "very nasty."

"He's put my officer's back up, so he doesn't like him, so that's a plus for us."

The officer called out, "Sergeant! Bring in the prisoner and let's hear what he has to say for himself."

"Sir, I'm acquainted with this man and I do not believe him to be a terrorist of any kind", the Sergeant interjected once inside the tent that was the Officers' Quarters.

"You'd better let me be the judge of that", the officer said, "we had better hear his story first, and let that other bright monkey cool off for a while. I do hate to be threatened, especially by a jumped-up civilian who thinks because they have a relation or friend in high office they can be above the law." He paused, "Right, Sergeant. You say you can vouch for this man who is accused of being a terrorist?"

"Yes Sir", the Sergeant answered confidently.

"You know you've not had those stripes long, do you want to risk them?" the officer asked.

"If it's to get to the truth, Sir, then yes." The Sergeant said, "I can't wear them without the pride and principles they mean."

"Good, I like my sergeants with integrity, you will go far in this army, and like you, I'm not going to sell it short no matter what jumped up politician wants to pull strings. If you had said anything else, you would be a private and he would be on his way with this Wilson bloke", the officer said.

Just then a Medical Officer pushed his way through the tent entrance, looked at Jeff silently, got out some field dressings, gave him an injection of something through the sleeve of his dirty shirt, then started to dress the wound. He then said briefly, "the jabs for the pain", finished dressing the wound and left the tent just as silently.

"Thank you", Jeff said to the back of the M.O. as he left, then commented, "he doesn't say much", Jeff said.

"Never does, but a good man to have in a tight spot", the officer said, "just like all my men, hand-picked for their skills. We are an elite squad and I am proud of every one of them, but I don't tell them that, they have to earn their respect the hard way, but I will be with them through hell or high water, and they will do the same for me."

He then eyed Jeff up and down and added, "Right what's your story, and it had better be the truth or you'll wish you had not been born."

Jeff's wife, Karen, had always said, Jeff was clever enough to let people think he was stupid, as it put him at a great advantage, when people think you're stupid they overplay their hand, but this time he had to convince the Officer he was not stupid, nor was he a terrorist or a murderer. He was a concerned environment warrior, who had old school principles and when he gave his word it was cast in granite, plus he was prepared to stand and be counted.

Jeff took his time and relayed his part in the events up-to-date whilst the officer listened intently.

~ 0 ~

After the officer had listened to what Jeff had to say, he retorted, "now, If you are to be believed, you are the hero of these events, if not then you are the villain, and in all sorts of problems", the officer said, "on one side you could be genuine and be who you say you are, on the other hand, you could be this very clever leader of a fifth columnist unit trying to overthrow the stability of the country, now, I have to determine which, before I take this further."

The officer continued, now we had better listen to what this Wilson bloke has to say now he's had time to cool his heels.

He shouted out to the corporal that was outside the officer's quarters, to fetch in Wilson, "But bring him in under escort. Let's hear what he has to say, and then we can decide who will go to the glasshouse because one of you will be locked up for good, that I promise you."

"Sir," the Sergeant said to the officer, "I wish to make a comment."

"Not until I've heard both sides, then I will hear what you have to say, Sergeant."

The Sergeant insisted, "but Sir, it's very important to the facts in this case."

"OK, Sergeant if you insist, I will hear what you have to say, whilst we wait for this Wilson character to be fetched."

The Sergeant started to relay what he knew, "I first saw Jeff Baker, near our Head Quarters, the day after the explosion took place, he was covered in dust and was staggering out of a building we thought had been cleared. How he got out alive is nothing short of a miracle if I remember rightly, he had blood running down his head, and he looked awful, so I sent him to the First Aid Unit that had just been established."

"Well, Sir! You know I am due to get married soon?" the Sergeant added,

"What's that got to do with what's going on here?" the officer stormed at him.

"Well, Sir! My fiancée was the nurse that attended him at the First Aid Unit, to cut a long story short, my fiancée has a sister and sister's talk. This sister has a boyfriend, who is a Police Sergeant, and that same Police Sergeant helped send Jeff on the mission he has been trying to tell you about, but he can't give you any details, because they have been sworn to secrecy by the Police Sergeants brother who works directly for the Prime Minister."

"Do you think I came over in the last banana boat", the officer said to the Sergeant, "people like this Jeff character, are not trained to be involved in espionage, now, Wilson yes, you can see by just looking at him he is a nasty piece of work, but we will wait to see what pans out after we speak to Wilson? Till then I will be fair and keep an open mind."

They waited in silence whilst Wilson was escorted to the officer's tent, he entered, flanked by two soldiers and a corporal.

"Thank you", the officer said to his men, "stay in case you're needed." Then he turned to Wilson, "right, let's hear your side of the story, starting with who you are and why you're hunting this man like an animal."

"I don't answer to you", Wilson replied to the officer, "and I'll have your head for holding me under arrest, I know some very powerful people in powerful places that will bury you."

"Unless I get some civility out of you", the officer returned, "you'll be escorted back to where my men are holding you, and in a few days' time, if I see fit, I will ask you the same question again, If I get the same remark as I've just had, you'll go back there for a month, do I make myself clear? Because I don't give a pigs' fart who you are, who you know, or how powerful they are, you will have respect for the rank I have earned it, so don't threaten me or my rank, do I make myself clear?"

Wilson looked stunned. He was used to giving orders, always using bullying tactics and thereby making others kowtow to his wishes, but here was someone that could not and would not be bullied.

"Ok, but I'll be making a report to Sir William" Wilson snapped.

"You can make a report to the Queen", the officer retorted forcefully, "I don't care, but until I hear all about what is going on, you're going nowhere and speaking to no-one, also, I'll put you under arrest permanently, do you understand me?"

"I hear, but Sir William is going to hear about this", Wilson said to the officer, "this man you have here is a terrorist and you're harbouring him, so you can be charged with treason and are in as much trouble as he is."

"Corporal", the officer said, "escort this man back to where you had him, no-one is to see or speak to him or his men for seven days, they're to be kept in isolation until I say otherwise."

"You can't do that", Wilson blustered, "you can't keep me locked up, on what grounds?"

"I'll think of something …. Maybe you and your men went through a contaminated area, and now you have to be isolated", the officer said, "I can hold on any darn charge I like, do you understand me?, or am I going to hear the truth from you now, without the threats, it's either that or I will have you locked away for good?"

"All right", Wilson suddenly capitulated, but remember, "he's considered to be a terrorist and you'll be held responsible for him."

"I'll be the judge of that, not you", the officer said, "so let's hear your version of events before I lose my patience."

Wilson went on to explain that he was Sir Williams' right-hand man. He boasted that Sir William would be the next leader of the country and under his dictatorship, only the purebred people would rule. He went on, to accuse Jeff of being the leader in a terrorist organization.

He told a story of how Jeff had plotted the explosion in the Lower Estuary by using suicide terrorists to act as Pirates, to high-jack, board, and capture a sea-going gas tanker, the pirates used the Somalian pirate's method of attacking ships, they approached the tanker from the stern by using rope ladders fired from a launcher, over the rails of the stern of the ship, climb the ladders and capture the gas ship, then these pirates had sent a message to Sir William Waits' offices demanding a ransom of £20 Million for the crew, the ship, and its cargo of Liquid Gas. But if the ransom was not paid, they would release the gas and blow up the ship.

But, before a rescue plan could be put into operation, they had sailed up the river and had blown up the ship. which in turn devastated the Estuary area.

Wilson then explained to the officer in detail what he thought had happened when the terrorists had manipulated the valves on the gas tanker, therefore pumping the Liquid Natural Gas into the river. He explained that because of this Liquid Natural Gas (LNG) is so cold (below minus 270 F or 160 C) the liquid will expand 620 times its volume into gas form instantly, which was known as Rapid Phase Transition (RPT), he added, it is like dropping an ice cube into boiling water because the ice can't expand into liquid and heat to boiling point instantly it explodes.

Wilson then explained that the gas formed at such a rate it caused the ship to explode with such a force, that in turn it spread to the area, blew up the Gas Terminal and the rest of the Estuary industries and then spread across and in turn created the domino effect disaster in the Estuary which in turn had killed thousands of people.

He added, Jeff was the leader of the terror cell, and Jeff was responsible, Wilson then sat back looking very smug, hoping what he had said stitched Jeff up for good.

At that point, Jeff reached inside his coat pocket, pulled out the papers he had been carrying and put them on the table. "These will prove otherwise", he said.

The look of horror on Wilson's face was a picture as he saw the incriminating evidence, he had been looking for on the table in front of him.

Wilson knew he had been outmanoeuvred, and he knew he desperately had to find a way out of this situation that had turned so badly against him so quickly. He realised he had been outmanoeuvred by an amateur. He had treated Jeff like he was stupid, it then dawned on him Jeff was only silly on his own side.

Jeff said," read those papers and the ones in the green Jag we stole from them that they were going to burn. My friend is trying to get to one of your units as we speak with the rest of these incriminating papers in that green Jag."

The officer started to read the papers in front of him, and then he ordered the corporal to radio all units to look out for the Jag and for it to be stopped and brought to the camp. They were also to capture Derek but not to harm him but to tell him that the troops were being sent by Jeff for a safe passage for him.

The corporal left to carry out his orders.

The officer continued reading the papers again, and then said to Wilson, holding them up so he could see, "this is very damning evidence for you and your people, Wilson."

With that remark, Wilson reacted fast. He dropped his hand to his right sock and pulled out the knife he had hidden there and lunged towards Jeff, shouting, "You bastard, I said I'd have you."

Jeff was slow to react to Wilson's lightning moves and did not move fast enough to avoid the knife completely. Even though Jeff moved to one side, Wilson still managed to stab him in the stomach as the soldiers escorting Wilson grabbed hold of him and wrestled him to the ground very roughly and with great difficulty.

"Get the MO here fast", the officer shouted to the sergeant, and then said to Wilson, "you've just proved your own guilt", pointing at Jeff, "if he dies, you can add the charge of murder, to your list of crimes. Escort, take him away."

"How the hell did he get that knife?" he said to the escorts that were pinning Wilson down.

"Don't know, sir", one of them answered struggling to hold Wilson.

Jeff felt a searing pain in his stomach and a warm sticky feeling oozing from the wound. The feeling went out of his legs and he sank to the ground, the sounds of people talking went very woolly, then he felt a searing pain in his temple and everything went dark.

~ 0 ~

Jeff came to in a makeshift Army Medical Unit. He was on a drip being fed into his arm, his stomach was very painful and sore and his head hurt like hell.

"About time you joined us", a voice said.

Jeff turned his head and there was Cyril and Jen looking down on him smiling. Cyril said, "We only came to see the big man here", pointing at the next bed where Derek lay sleeping. "He was battered and bruised but patched up and wrapped in bandages, but you were here also, so we had to come and say hello to you as well", Cyril said wryly.

Cyril's face changed as he said, "Wilson got away. He killed one of the soldiers, slightly wounded that officer, stole a jeep, and crashed through a cordon. He must have thought he left you for dead, and that sergeant is in a right mood over his men not searching Wilson properly" he said, "he was going to fry the balls of the man who supposed to have searched him."

Jen said, "your stomach wound isn't too bad, but apparently it bled a lot. Wilson missed any vital organs, you have three broken ribs, and that bash on your temple when you hit the table probably put you out." "Maybe it knocked some sense into you, and by the way you have a flesh wound from a bullet.

See, I can't leave you alone for 5 minutes without you getting into some sort of trouble?" Jen added, with a smile.

Jeff turned to Cyril and said, "Sorry about Alan."

"He had it coming from what Derek told me. I didn't realise how selfish Alan had become and how money orientated he was. Derek made sure I knew before I saw you, which was before they operated on him to remove the two bullets Alan put into him."

"I knew he was hit once, I didn't know he was hit twice", Jeff said, "He never told me."

"He wouldn't", Cyril said, "Jen asked him to look after you, and he did, I know how he feels about Jen, but there's nothing I can do about that, and I wouldn't hurt him for the world."

"The man has a heart as big as he is", Jeff said.

"Unfortunately for Derek, Jen loves me. She is very fond of Derek, but there could never be anything between them, and like me, she would not hurt him. He'll take a while to heal, but he will mend alright, you can't keep a man like him down for long", Cyril said.

"So, what's happening out there now?" Jeff asked, "How did you get here? How did you get past the troopers? What happened to everybody? The last thing Alan told me was you were all going to be rounded up and either shot or interned for good."

"One question at a time but slowly", Jen said, "you've been out for nearly two days, you must have bumped your head pretty hard, so take it slow over a cup of tea."

"You and your tea", Jeff said, "you would cure the world's ills over a cup of tea."

"Well it does help", Jen said, "let's try to bring you up to speed, but I warn you I will stop if you get tired."

Jen explained, "We made our way to the golf course, meeting the others as we went along as we approached the course we heard shots being fired from the direction that you went in, this made us suspicious, so Cyril put out scouts, and they spotted the ambush, the troopers started to open fire on us before we were in their trap.

Just as we returned fire, two lorry loads of soldiers turned up, they were from your mate John, they surrounded the squad of troopers, then spoke to the leader of the troopers, they laid down their weapons and then they were rounded up, put in the lorries and taken away.

The soldiers escorted us out of the area, so the clean-up teams could go in. By the way, they talked of nobody being able to live there, and the whole area being used as a memorial to the dead from this disaster."

Jen looked at Jeff intently, and said, "you're getting tired, we'll go now, but we will bring you up-to-date later after you've had some rest."

As they left Jen said, "by the way, we met you're mate John, on the way here. He said he will see you later after he's done some cleaning up."

When they'd both left a nurse came in to look after him and then fussed a lot over Derek.

He slowly drifted off to sleep, his mind in a whirl, trying to piece together all that had happened in such a short time.

He awoke later with his wife Karen sitting beside his bed, and his daughter was talking to Derek.

They both saw he was awake at the same time and leaned over to cuddle him hard, then said together, "we are not letting you out of our sight ever again."

"Good job you decided to take your mum to the spa when you did", Jeff said, to his daughter, "holding her hand tightly."

Karen said, "we've been under that John's protection ever since they picked us up from the spa", she said, "how he knew we were there I don't know, but we can't move without an escort of at least two armed men, I've been worried sick about you and this terrible accident. Can you tell me how did it happen?"

before Jeff could reply to his wife, she said, "you were right, you said it was a disaster waiting to happen, well it did. I hope they're happy now that they've destroyed a whole community" then she added, "All those people dead! What for? Greed and profit, it's terrible". She checked herself and said she was sorry for rambling on, but she had been so frightened.

Worst of all she said she felt so guilty that they had survived when so many others had died.

"What have you been up to?" Karen asked, then she promptly harped back to the issue at hand and added, "It's terrible what's happened to Derek, but I gather he will heal with that nurse looking after him", then Karen said, nervously, "I'm sorry, I keep rambling on, but I'm so relieved you're not dead", she hugged him hard enough to make him wince. She said she was sorry and hugged him again.

Just then the door opened and John walked in. Sorry to break up the reunion but we need to talk urgently.

Karen flew at John in a protective rage, "Can't you let him rest? Hasn't he done enough for you and the country?" Karen said angrily, then added, "You won't be satisfied until he's dead, then what do I do?" then on seeing Jeff's face, and knowing how strong his principles were, which was one of the reasons why she loved him so much, she stopped in mid-sentence. Karen resigned herself to the inevitable, then said, "I'll be outside when you've finished." She turned to John and said, "try not to tire him too much?"

"Well, what's the emergency?" Jeff asked John.

"Well", John said, "you know Wilson escaped, but we don't know where he is, he thought you were dead, but he's just found out you're still alive and is trying to get to you any way he can, so I've now put a cordon around this place. I'll be moving your wife and daughter into safe custody and a safe location as of now."

"Thank you for keeping your word and keeping them safe", Jeff said.

"Like you, I keep my word", John said.

Jeff said, "Whilst you're here you might as well bring me up to speed with what's happening with Sir William and his cronies? And what's happened to all the documents I got for you? What's happened to everyone who was in the area?"

Jeff continued, "What's happening about Cyril, Jen, Derek, Michael and all the others that have helped get those documents you so desperately wanted? And what's happening about the Terminal?"

"One question at a time", John said, "we had to stretch our resources pretty thinly to pull together all that we did in such a short time, luckily, the Prime Minister still has a few friends he can call on in a crisis."

Then John said, "one lesson Sir William never learned, you have to be careful of the toes you tread on the way up because they belong to the feet you have to kiss on the way down. In treading on those toes on the way up Sir William made a lot of enemies and they're having their day now, revenge is so sweet when served cold the PM said."

"We have Sir William. He is under arrest and is being held in a secure location awaiting trial. Those documents are being studied as we speak and from the initial reading, they will condemn Sir William, Wilson, a whole lot of councillors and planning officials and have far-reaching implications in Whitehall where heads are rolling.

Also, even more sinister, they are also trying to find out more about this right-wing group called "The Senate" that seems you unwittingly uncovered, and they seem to be the underlying cause of the instability because of these people in high places that are associated with this group are being instantly replaced."

John continued, "the approaches to the whole of the Estuary area have been sealed off and nobody is allowed into the area unless they have a written mandate from the PM, and only then, not until the

Health and Safety and the Disaster Recovery Team have done their investigation. All bodies are being respectfully removed, also they are being identified by the emergency services as best they can be, all of that will take some time, we are receiving a massive amount of aid from a lot of countries, especially America, and that aid is flooding in as we speak."

John Continued, "the PM has opened our borders to any humanitarian aid that has been offered, but most of all, there is a massive hue and cry in every country in the world to crush this group "The Senate" that seems to be undermining the stability of different countries by using the power of the global Energy Companies.

There is a massive outcry for all "Top Tier COMAH" sites, to be relocated away from any population." John added.

"It's a bit bloody late for that now", Jeff said, "It's bloody typical of politicians, never listen to the people's concerns, because everyone wants to get on the political gravy train of profit. They call people like me, anarchists, and trouble makers, as an excuse, so they don't have to listen to the truth. Then they wring their hands and cry, we didn't know when it all goes wrong.

It's not until thousands have to die", Jeff added, "a Government has been brought to its knees, comes to the brink of collapse, a whole region has to be devastated, the country has been put back into the dark ages, all to prove that common sense was right, and people come before profit, all the bloody politicians are worried about is their political image to the world and getting on the gravy train and feathering their own nests, not the views of the people who elected them into power."

Jeff added, "the only time they might listen to what people are saying is at election time when they are looking for that little cross that will give them a ticket to get them back onto the gravy train again, once they have got that, they put their feet back in the trough of profit."

"You're really cynical about politicians and politics", John said.

Jeff replied, "until they prove otherwise, I will always consider that politics and a lot of people that are involved in politics are what the word expresses "POLI- TICS", "POLI" is many, and "TICKS" are "PARASITES" therefore there are mostly parasites in politics."

John replied, "I heard you play that old record the first time."

Jeff changed the subject and asked, "What's going to happen to Cyril, Jen, Michael and all the others?

They're in a luxury hotel right now resting at our expense", John replied, "and they send their regards, by the way, we had to move them from the first hotel we put them up in, because some idiot put them in the same hotel as some of your local councillors, who in turn were boasting to the press over a civic lunch, how much they cared and how they were going to lead their community out of its crisis. When they heard that, Cyril, Jen and Michael were baying for their blood and they did not stay quiet like the councillors wanted them to, they created havoc and our security people had to intervene."

John added, "It's not done any of the councillors' image much good, and when Cyril told them and the press what you did, plus they also found out you are not dead, but very much alive, but injured, they've gone berserk, and have been camping outside ever since, just waiting for a statement and photoshoot with you. The Prime Minister will be coming to see you very soon so you can both talk about what you should say when you make a joint statement to the press, and then there could be an audience with the Queen in a few days' time."

"Are you and your political cronies trying to manipulate me?" Jeff asked, "because it won't work."

"No", John said, "but you must understand we are at a very delicate time politically, and we must be seen to be doing the right thing for the people, we just had this failed political coup by "The Senate", the biggest peacetime industrial disaster since the 2nd World War, with a death count that is still climbing, the people need to believe in someone, the people need a champion to look to that they can trust, and you're the nearest we have got."

"I've never been a glory hunter, so I'll pass on that, thank you very much", Jeff said dismissively.

"You are such a self-righteous bastard", John snapped angrily, "if you don't do it for yourself, do it for the people who believe in you. Do it for the Cyril's, the Jen's, the Michael's, and the Derek's of this world. It's them that need something to believe in at this time of monumental crisis, and you're that something whether you want to be it, or not."

Jeff sat quietly, contemplating, then said "O.K." very reluctantly, "but if he's going to talk a load of politics I'll get up and walk out from the press conference, I want action, not political promises that will be expediently withdrawn at the next political crisis."

"Be reasonable Jeff, you can't dictate to a Prime Minister what you want. Not when he's come to praise you in front of the world."

"Alright", Jeff said, "but I don't have to like it."

"When is this conference going to take place? And will the others be there?"

"In a little while", John said, "Derek will have to have his nurse with him, but the others will be at the press conference and photo call as well as yourself and the Prime Minister."

"You don't give a man a lot of time to make himself good looking?" Jeff joked.

"There's not that much time in the world to make you good looking", John said, "plus, there is not enough scaffold to give you a face lift", he laughingly added.

"Cyril, Jen, and Michael are already there, we have just enough time to get you and Derek spruced up", and he left.

~ 0 ~

They were waiting in the wings, waiting for the signal to enter the forum.

Derek's nurse was hovering over Derek like a little angel and he had only eyes for her. It was lovely to see a great big man reduced to a jelly by the pretty nurse, who obviously liked him an awful lot.

"Do we hear wedding bells?" Jen asked smiling and looking at the nurse and Derek.

"Aw Jen", Derek said, very bashfully, "you know I'll always have a soft spot for you."

"We know", Cyril said, "you can be best man at our wedding unless you want to make it a double wedding? or is it too soon?"

Derek just coloured up and the nurse kissed him, and said, "It's up to you, big boy, I know what I want, and it's right here in my arms."

Just then, they got instructed to go on stage. They went on from the left-hand side, the Prime Minister came on from the right-hand side and greeted them in the middle shaking their hands one by one, as they took their seats.

The Prime Minister started the press conference by saying how sad he was at the loss of life and he wanted his heartfelt condolences given to all the suffering families of the people who died.

The Prime Minister also announced the forthcoming trial of Sir William Waits and why he was being put on trial. He also spoke openly of the right-wing group called the "Senate" and how they had manipulated the situation to try to take over the country.

The P.M. then fielded questions on what was happening in the disaster recovery area and how many estimated deaths there had been, plus, he promised a full and frank investigation into the events and that the findings of that investigation would be made public and any recommendations carried out.

The P.M. told the press of the parts played by Cyril, Jen, Michael, Derek and mostly Jeff and then asked for questions from the reporters and television interviewers.

The Prime Minister fielded most of the questions very well, but one reporter kept asking the same question, will you change your energy policy, to a "safe siting policy" for Top Tier COMAH sites, but the Prime Minister kept ignoring it, and then the same reporter asked the Prime Minister, "What lessons had been learned from all this devastation and massive loss of life?"

The Prime Minister replied that everything that was humanly possible was being done for the victims. He also added that Investigations were going on into the causes of the terrible disaster and life would be returned to order in the area as soon as possible.

Then the reporter, repeated the same question, "yes, Prime Minister that is all very well, but can you tell us what lessons have been and were being learned from this major incident?"

Jeff's frustration of the P.M. political dodging the question got the better of him, he leapt to his feet and said, "None."

The Prime Minister looked embarrassed and shocked at Jeff's interruption.

The whole room went quiet for a few moments. John looked on in shocked horror from the wings then indicated silently by putting his hand across his throat in a slicing motion that Jeff should shut up and not embarrass the P.M.

Then there was a buzz of voices from the reporters demanding to know what he had meant by the remark.

The Prime Minister could see what was billed as a hero's welcome celebration, that was also to gain him popularity, was now falling apart and was turning into a political nightmare in front of the press.

He spoke directly to Jeff and started to bluster about costs and time required to find causes and then to make the right recommendations.

Jeff turned to the Prime Minister and said coldly, "there have been recommendations made in the past, but no-one wants to learn any lessons from all the accidents involving Top Tier COMAH sites, they don't want to hear any recommendations from the investigations into those accidents, when reminded of them at planning stage they finish up only being recommendation that is not implemented."

Jeff added, "the reason is that it would affect the profits of the companies and the financial implications for the governments concerned until there is a "safe siting policy" for all Top Tier COMAH sites strictly that is strictly adhered to, there will always be the threat of this sort of accident happening again."

"We will give assurances that everything that can be done will be done", the Prime Minister said trying to rescue the situation.

"That's not good enough", Jeff said, "you have a paper tiger with no teeth in place at the moment." then turning to the Prime Minister again, "I want you to guarantee to the media (pointing to the press), that you and future governments of Great Britain will adopt a safe siting policy for all Top Tier COMAH site areas, starting now."

Jeff emphasised, "If not, all those people died for nothing, the memory of the horror of inside that school will be burned on my memory forever, either move people away from within the cordon of safety surrounding these terminals or relocate these terminals to a safer location, also, never allow any planning of any sort within a 4-mile radius of these types of terminals. Also, you need to openly encourage those companies to own the land within that Cordon Sanitaire or Safety Zone and for it to be kept as a safety buffer zone, and not built on for any reason, plus encourage all other countries throughout the world to do the same."

The Prime Minister looked at Jeff, smiled, and said, "I know now where you get your reputation, Thank god you're not in politics."

Jeff ignored the soft soap remark, that was meant to appease him.

"You must adopt this type of policy as of now", Jeff said, "otherwise all these deaths were for nothing, and you'll be accused as being as bad as Sir William."

The Prime Minister gauged the political situation instantly, then stood up and addressed the media, saying to Jeff, "I'm willing to embrace all your suggestions and any more safety recommendations that come out of the investigations into this accident in memory of those poor souls who have died",

Jeff stood and said, "your promise will be good enough for me but remember, I will be looking over your shoulder to make sure you carry out that promise for the people."

The Prime Minister, not slow in using a political advantage said to Jeff in front of the media, "how about you putting your money where your mouth is? how about you heading that team under a Royal Commission?"

Jeff was astounded and did not know what to say, he was lost for words.

The Prime Minister stated, "this team will be funded by the Government, plus it will be totally independent of government intervention, you can even choose your own staff and teams to work with, your recommendations will be adhered to, What do you say?" knowing he had outmanoeuvred Jeff.

"Well?" The PM asked, "would you do it? Or are you all talk?"

Jeff knew, whether he liked it or not, that he had been outmanoeuvred by the PM and nodded, said yes and leaned across and shook the Prime Minister's hand.

The press and the media people cheered and there was a burst of pictures taken by the press and TV cameras.

As they were shaking hands, the Prime Minister whispered to Jeff, I leave them to you, pointing to the media and left the press conference the way he had come in, leaving Jeff to face a lot of questions on how he was going to fulfil his new job from the press, and also barrage photographers.

The PM said to John, as they left the press conference, "I think I might just have contained our loose cannon by bringing him into the fold."

John said, "If you want my advice, which you don't if Jeff does not get his own way on this, he could be a major problem to you politically."

"It's in our political interest at the moment, to let the media and him believe what we have just said", the P.M. remarked.

He added, "the energy crisis that will be developing around the world will dictate the way we perceive the situation in ten years' time, but for now I need to secure myself politically and then get this country back onto its feet. If playing lip service to this Jeff bloke and the media achieves that then that is to the good."

"You could be sowing dragon's teeth", John remarked to the P.M., "just like out of that book, Jason and the Argonauts."

"Someone once said, a week is a long time in politics", the PM said.

"My main concern at the moment is keeping this Jeff bloke alive, and not being killed by that killer Wilson, because if Wilson kills Jeff or a member of his family dies, not of natural causes shall we say, the other papers that you did not find, will, I am assured, find their way to the press, and I don't want that to happen, that could be very embarrassing to me and the whole of the newly to be elected Government."

"Do you mean to say you're in on all this intrigue?" John asked, slowing his steps.

"Its politics!", the P.M. said, "you can't be totally blind in this game."

"A game? That's all it is to you?" John said, "a bloody game?"

"You know Jeff was right", John added, "when he described politics as POLI is many and TICKS were parasites, he described politicians as MANY PARASITES."

"That's a good analogy", the PM said totally un-phased, "I must remember to quote that sometimes", then added, "you find those papers that Jeff has squirrelled away, and then we are off the hook, but until then we play politics."

"I didn't know there were other incriminating papers", John said. Then he added, "What do they contain? And where do I start looking?"

"I understand the papers we are talking about were in that Councillor Randle's safe", the PM said, "where they are now, I don't know, but Jeff was the last one to raid that safe, so he must have them or know where they are.

At the moment he is untouchable because of the press interest in him and what he does, that's why I brought him into the fold where we might be able to keep an eye on him, and at least have some control over him without him knowing."

"He's not likely to tell me where he's put them, or even if he has them", John said, "it could take some time to gain his confidence enough for him to trust me and then to tell me where these papers are."

"That has to be your Prime Ministerial Commission to carry out, and it must be treated with priority", the PM said, "I will give you the written authority, and you'll only report directly to me is that clear?"

"Yes," said John, "I'd better start now, and go back in there and rescue him from the press. You never know, he could get popular."

"That's my worry", the PM said, "I don't want him as popular as myself or my political party at this stage, we can't afford loose cannons flying around that we have no control over."

"The one thing I learned about Jeff", John said, "is that he is someone you can't control. Oh, you can lead him around by a ring through his nose like a tame bull, and with the right kind of handling, but he is so stubborn, if you try to push him in a direction he does not want to go in, you come up against a solid lump of granite that won't budge", John continued, "he can be led, but he cannot be driven, and if he finds out you lie to him, he shuts up like a clam, and then you will never get anything out of him."

"A man of principles", the P.M. said, "that's rare today, but a man of principles must have a weakness somewhere. It's up to you to get on his good side and find it, now I must go, I'm late for my next meeting, go and try to control our new loose cannon, but above all at this moment in time, keep him safe."

The P.M. added as a parting shot, "don't forget that killer Wilson is still out there somewhere and he hates Jeff with a passion and will try to get to him by any means fair or foul."

Meanwhile, back at the press conference with Jeff deliberately taking a back seat, Jen, Cyril, Michael and Derek were answering questions about their part in their survival and the incidents involving Sir William's men.

One of the reporters said to Derek, "So, it was you that was the hero that rescued those two girls we heard about, and the people at the sports center when they believed they were going to be lined up and shot."

Derek said, "It wasn't just only me, Jeff was there and did most of it", he said shyly.

His nurse snuggled up to him, indicating to everybody who was there that Derek belonged to her, and she cared deeply for him, and then said, "yes, he was a real hero."

"A Code to Live or Die by"

They all faced questions, on all the different incidents that had transpired, but the press had left Jeff until last and started questioning him about what had happened leading up to, during, and after the industrial accident.

There was a sea of flashing cameras, all of the photographers were lifting their cameras up to their faces to take their photos, then looking at their cameras to get the settings right, then repeating the action to take another or better shot.

But there was one cameraman during the interviews with the other press media, he kept his camera up hiding his face all the time, but also he did not seem to be taking any pictures, but slowly making his way to the front through the crowd of photographers, that were all jostling one another for the best photographs.

Jeff noticed this was happening, because he was not fielding any questions at the time, and he thought this very strange, as there was all this press and camera activity going on but this man was not taking pictures.

It was then that he realised who the cameraman was. It was Wilson, and he was hiding a gun inside the camera and heading straight for them.

"That's Wilson", Jeff shouted, "and he has a gun", pointing in Wilson's direction. Jeff dived on top of Cyril, Michael, Derek and Jen bringing them to the ground in a heap behind the desks they were standing in front of, just as Wilson fired his gun.

Wilson's eyes, were the eyes of a maniac, and he was screaming, "I thought you were dead, well you are now. And as for the rest of you bastards, you're dead too. I said I'd get you too."

Jeff heard a fuselage of shots and felt a searing pain in his side, leg and chest all one after the other.

Jeff knew that he had been hit badly, then everything started to fade, with voices that seemed as though they were talking in a tunnel, then it went dark.

Wilson was gunned down in a hail of bullets, from the secret service gunmen that appeared from nowhere, in the crossfire three photographers were wounded.

Behind the desk Cyril, Michael, Derek, Jen and Jeff lay tumbled together with blood all over them, people rushed forward to help them.

"I'm alright", Jen said struggling to her feet.

"So, am I", Michael said, "except for a nick in the arm", he held his arm out which was bleeding profusely.

"Well, he didn't get me or Sandra, Derek said", checking his little nurse to see if she was alright.

"He got me in the leg", Cyril said holding his thigh.

Then Jen said, "so then where's all this blood from?"

It was then that they saw Jeff sprawled unconscious in a heap on the floor bleeding from his leg, side and chest.

"Oh no!", Jen said, falling to her knees at Jeff's side, then shouted for someone to get an ambulance fast.

The paramedics arrived instantly, as they were always on standby where ever the P.M. was, and they went to work on Jeff straight away, telling the security staff to move everybody out so they could do their job.

There was a bevvy of photographs being taken by photographers as they were being herded out of the room by the security staff.

The inquest on how Wilson got past security with a camera gun, would be held later by John.

In the meanwhile, John had three wounded press photographers to get hospitalised in one hospital, he had to get Derek and his nurse, Jen, Michael and Cyril in a more secure hospital, he had already notified that same hospital to clear the operating table for an emergency gunshot wound surgery for Jeff in the hope he would make it in time but from the look of it he did not hold out much hope.

The paramedics, however, were working hard to stabilise him so he could be moved to the hospital and an operating theatre. "We can move him now", the paramedic said, "he's stable for now."

They moved him to a waiting ambulance with Jen clucking over the stretcher and an unconscious Jeff like a mother hen, and woe betide anyone who got in their way, she took no prisoners.

Everything sounded woolly to Jeff as he gradually came round, he could see more clearly as each moment passed, he felt very restricted as though he was in a straight jacket and had been run over by a steam roller.

As things started to clear he saw Karen sitting by his bedside looking very worried, he said in a croaking voice, "Hi lovely."

Karen burst into tears, but at the same time, she was smiling. She said, "you had me worried, I can't leave you alone for five minutes without you getting up to some sort of mischief", then she kissed and hugged him.

Karen, brought him up to speed with what had happened. She said that some of the others had been hit but they were alright now, and they were up itching to see him. She told him that John had returned to the press conference room just as Wilson had opened fire, and how John had hit Wilson with three shots stopping him instantly.

Karen, also told him of some spectacular footage taken by a television crew of Jeff diving across the others when Wilson attacked and it was being shown on the television throughout the world.

Jeff started to get tired, so she said she would let him get some sleep and be back later. He was already drifting off into a peaceful sleep as she was going out of the door.

Later Jeff was sitting up in his bed, in the private ward he had been given. He had just had his dressings changed and the doctor had commented that he was doing very well and could have a few visitors.

John came in and said, "I can see you're on the mend, at last, well, I have some very good news for you."

"I've been trying to find out what happened to your boys, and I've found your youngest one, he was on holiday with his family in Spain, your eldest son, was with his in-laws in Scotland, so they're all safe."

Jeff thanked him for the news through tearful eyes of happiness.

John left, saying he would see him very soon, just to bring him up to speed with everything. John also told him that due to all the publicity that he had got, it now meant he could not do any of his undercover work, and the P.M. had said that he was to be promoted and appointed to Jeff, as his personal bodyguard.

As John left, Jen, Michael with his arm in a bandage, followed by Derek and his nurse Sandra who never left his side and then Cyril who was hobbling on a stick, they all tumbled into the room.

"You had us worried for a while there", Jen said.

"I've never seen her in such a state as she was over you", Cyril said, "and that photographer who got in the way, and tried to stop the stretcher, just so he could get a picture will be eating through a straw for a month, she gave him such a right hook when he would not get out of the paramedics' way, so they could get you to hospital."

"Stupid man", Jen said, "fancy trying to stop someone getting life-saving attention just so they can get a picture for their paper."

"Remind me never to stand in your way when you're angry", Derek said smiling, "I like my teeth too much."

Michael said jokingly, "even I wouldn't upset her when she's angry."

"Hey, I'm not that bad", Jen said defensively then burst out laughing.

"What do you mean?", Cyril laughed with her and said, "we are getting you a rematch with Tyson."

With that remark, Jen whacked Cyril on the arm.

"See what I mean", Cyril said in mock hurt.

"Shut up", Jen said, "we're here to see our blood brother."

"Who's your blood brother?" Jeff asked.

"You are", Jen replied. "When you needed a few pints of blood to stop you bleeding like a stuck pig, it turned out Derek and myself were the same blood type as you, so whether you like it or not you got our blood in you, by the way, you also got some from that John bloke as well."

Derek said, "that John bloke gave you blood?" then added, "do you know what his last name is? It's Stone, so you actually got blood out of a stone."

They all laughed together.

"Stop making me laugh, you're making my stitches hurt", Jeff gasped.

Cyril said, "the doc says you might be out of here soon, so when you're up and about, Jen and I would like you to be the best man at our wedding."

"You two are getting married?", Jeff said, "that's great news, when?"

"As soon as you're well enough", Jen said.

Derek said, "Can you make it two weddings?" Looking moonstruck at Sandra his nurse.

"Why not make it a double wedding?" Jen suggested, looking at Sandra, and then added, "that's if you don't mind."

"That would be the icing on the cake for me if that happened", Sandra said.

"Icing, Wedding cake", Michael remarked, "what a pun."

They all laughed together.

~ 0 ~

EPILOGUE

A few weeks later, John was in a meeting with the P.M. and some other Cabinet Ministers.

As the meeting finished and they were going out of the door John overheard one of the Ministers say to the P.M. …. "a bit fortunate that Wilson exposed himself when he did, otherwise you could have been diving out of his way for years to come, knowing how good a reputation that man had for being a professional killer. Good job your man here was better", he said tapping John on the shoulder, "then left the meeting."

When all the Ministers had gone, John started mulling these comments over in his mind and a few things did not add up.

So, John confronted the P.M. "How come Wilson knew of and was prepared for that press conference in advance? He couldn't have got a camera gun at that short notice without alarm bells ringing somewhere? You were the one to call that press conference and you chose the venue?" With unbelievable comprehension dawning inside his head, John said, "it was you that let Wilson know about that press conference, so you could bring him out of hiding, hoping I would kill him in a shootout."

"Well, you did, didn't you?" the P.M. rejoined.

"What would have happened if I had missed?" John asked.

"Well instead of being in that Jeff's debt", the P.M. added, "I would have been in Wilson's debt", the P.M. continued, "do you know how they used to trap and kill tigers in India years ago?"

"What's that got to do with the situation?'", John asked.

"Well", said the P.M. "when they trap tigers, they leave a goat tethered to a tree and lie in wait for the tiger to attack the goat and then they kill the tiger if they can", then he added, "sometimes the tiger wins and gets the goat and sometimes he doesn't."

"How could you do something like that?" John asked the P.M. not hiding his disgust.

"Wilson forgot the basic rules in your profession", the P.M stated, "Don't get emotionally involved with your target, so, I counted on Wilson's hate of Jeff to override his professionalism and go for the kill with such a passion that he would expose himself enough so you could take him down."

"What about Jeff and the others? Did they know you had set them up?" John asked.

"They don't have to know; it would spoil their sense of adventure in the life of politics", the P.M. replied.

John walked away disgusted and said, "Thank Christ I am not a politician!"

~ 0 ~

Lightning Source UK Ltd.
Milton Keynes UK
UKHW020820020820
367542UK00004B/45